The Way
the Family
Got
Away

The Way
the Family
Got
Away

Michael Kimball

Fourth Estate • London

First published in Great Britain in 2000 by
Fourth Estate Limited
6 Salem Road
London W2 4BU
www.4thestate.co.uk

1 3 5 7 9 10 8 6 4 2

A catalogue record for this book
is available from the British Library.

ISBN 1-84115-208-0

Typeset by MATS, Southend-on-Sea, Essex
Printed in Great Britain by T.J. International Ltd, Padstow, Cornwall

For Bompa

Contents

The baby lived inside a world that was smaller and older where they still traveled by carriage and spoke a bawling language.

Bompa

The bawling language was small and died inside the baby and inside the bodies of everybody who could hear it.

Bompa

whah whaahh uuhhh
dahhh dadadadada
mabadaduwigo

My Little Brother

The Whole Way We Got There

My brother's cradle and other baby stuff got us from Mineola to Birthrock. My mother's necklaces and other dress-up stuff got us from Birthrock to Stringtown. This girl there got my sister's doll people along with all the other things that went with her practice family. They told my sister she wasn't going to need her dollhouse and the doll people living in it anymore since we weren't living in our house anymore. So my sister's dollhouse and everything in it got us from Stringtown to Albion. That was where this other man got my father's pocketwatch and pocketknife along with some other things my father almost always kept with him whenever we went anywhere.

Those things from my father's pockets got us from Albion and all the way out of Oklahoma to Hot Springs and our start through Arkansas. That was where this other boy got my baseball bat and baseball glove along with some other things they told me were too small for me. This other boy got all my clothes but for the handed-down-to-me suit of clothes they made me wear and that left me with a ways to go before it would fit me. My brother might have gotten the baseball stuff handed-down-to-him along with the clothes but he wasn't ever going to grow up into any of it anyway.

So all my stuff got us from Hot Springs to North Little Rock and we stopped for that one night. That was where these other people got our pillows, blankets, sheets, and the other stuff that helped us sleep. We got from North Little Rock to Campbell Station and we kept going away. My mother's purse along with everything she had left in it got us from Campbell Station to Biggerton. This other girl there got my sister's locket and chain that had a picture of my sister in it from when she was a baby and sick. But my sister did not die from that and that other girl getting it and that locket and chain still got us out of Biggerton and Arkansas and into Glenallen in Missouri. That was where these other men got my father's wallet along with all the stuff my father had left in his wallet. There were the family pictures of us and the cards that had the names of other people and other places on them. There wasn't any money left but we didn't need any money anymore anyway. My father's wallet along with all the stuff left in it got us from Glenallen to Anna, Illinois and left us in the middle of America with all those miles behind us and all those miles to go farther away in front of us.

Anna was where this other boy got my guns, my holster belt, and all the bullets that went in my gun or went in the loops of my holster belt and around my waist. My guns and other play stuff got us from Anna to Giantsburg and Old Shawneetown, over the Ohio River, all the way out of Illinois, and up into the hump of Kentucky that has Henderson in it. That was where my mother traded her wedding dress and wedding ring away to this other lady that wanted to wear them and get married. That other lady also wanted the veil to the wedding dress but my mother didn't have it or any of her other wedding things left but my father. But my mother's wedding things still got those two other people married and us from Henderson to Hendricksville. This girl there got all my sister's clothes but for the dress my sister put on to wear out of Hendricksville, up through Six Points, Big Sheridan, Russellville, and into Bennetts Switch.

It was there that we got down to where my mother's clothes were almost the last stuff of hers that anybody else really wanted and that got us from Bennetts Switch to Frederick Perrytown. This other brother and sister there got the record player and records that my sister and me played in the back seat. The record player and records made somebody up out of words and songs but trading them away also got us out of Frederick Perrytown, out of Indiana, and up into Edwardsburg at the beginning of Michigan.

All this stuff so far got us up to where this man got the silver frame with the picture of our whole family in it—the picture that had all the old people in it that were already dead and some others of us that weren't dead yet. Our family was going to need everybody we had left in it to get there. That silver frame with the family picture and all those dead people and us got us the miles that got us out of Edwardsburg, up through Schoolcraft, over to Battle Creek, and into Sunfield. That was where this other father and his family got our suitcases and the

3

other things where we had packed our stuff up. Those suitcases, boxes, and crates were almost empty anyway and that other father and his family let us keep the things we had left in them—the underwear and the shoes, the doll parts, our dirty clothes, and some other stuff of ours that nobody else ever wanted but us. My brother was the only empty thing that we kept with us.

But there was all that other stuff that wasn't ours anymore. There was that other family on their way to somewhere else. There was all our other stuff with all those other people and other families all over America. But all this stuff so far also got us out of Sunfield, into and out of Lyons and Hubbardston, and up into Far Town. These other people there got everything we had left in the glove box—the maps and our other car papers, the flashlight, a pair of sunglasses, some batteries, a sewing kit, a first-aid kit, some gloves, and some other small things that fit in there. All that stuff from the glove box got us all the way out of Far Town and up into Morrison. That was where there were some men along the way that took our spare tire along with the hubcaps, the tire jack, the lug wrench, and some other tools that were in the trunk. Those men took our back seat for the back of their pickup truck and took our rearview mirror so they could see if anybody else was sitting down in it. The rest of our car got us up through Marceytown and Roscommon, on through Toms Mile, Bradford, and some other places that got their names from people that must have done stuff. Or maybe people got that far and then just stopped so that the town and everybody else kept growing up out of all

4

those miles. We stopped in Gaylord and kept going—into its streets and up to the two-story house that was going to have Bompa coming out of it to take us inside it.

That was as far as all that stuff got us. There were all those towns that we stopped at and all those towns that we did not stop at until we got to Gaylord. We traded for the next town in Hot Springs and in Anna, in Henderson and in Frederick Perrytown, in places that never got big enough to get a name, and in all the other towns along the way that already had their names. We traded our stuff away for miles. We traded for the lives of other people, what might have happened to us for what did.

Living Anymore in Mineola

My brother's fever wouldn't leave him or us and our house. My mother took how hot my brother was from out of his mouth but his fever didn't go down. She rubbed ice cubes on his forehead and lips that melted on her fingers and dried on her hands and his face and he cried. My brother reached his small hands up to his face and shook his head back and forth and pushed away from us. He wouldn't look at us or our family.

We weren't supposed to go into my brother's room anymore or he wouldn't get any better than he was then. His whole room was sick. His body swelled up and made his cradle rock back and forth and rattle. My mother and father and sister and me all stood in the doorway to his sickroom where we could still look at him. My sister told us that we had to stop the cradle from rocking back and forth or my brother might tip over and fall and break. My sister went into my brother's sickroom and carried my brother out of there and through all the other rooms of the house that weren't sick or dying or small but we still had to go to the hospital.

My brother was going to die. We drove him down a road that wasn't big enough to be paved yet but that had men standing next to it hammering nails into houses so other families would come and live there. We drove past the school where my sister was supposed to go with me next year but where she never did. We drove past stores and gas stations and places to eat but none of them had anything in them that would keep my brother alive.

We drove my brother to the hospital that had the doctor and nurse that were supposed to save my brother for us. My mother told the doctor and nurse that we starved my brother but even so his fever didn't go down. The nurse fixed the table paper up and the doctor laid my brother down on it and on top of the metal table. The doctor looked inside my brother's ears and mouth and down his throat. He pulled my brother's eyelids up with his thumb but they closed up again when he let go of them. My brother squeezed his eyes down tight into wrinkles and cried. He shook his head back and forth so the doctor couldn't put anything else in his mouth and the doctor put his hands down into his pockets and he frowned.

My brother stopped breathing anymore but his body was still hot when we touched him. My sister pulled her hand back fast and told me it burned. The nurse breathed out into my brother's mouth and pushed down on his chest with her two fingers. My brother coughed and spit and cried. My mother and father cried too. My brother reached his small hands and arms out to us and my mother picked him up and held him in our family.

We took my brother away from the hospital alive but we didn't get very far away before my brother stopped breathing again and we took him back home. My mother carried my brother into our house but he wasn't going to live there or with us anymore. But we had to keep living even though my brother wasn't going to do it.

We stayed inside our family and house and got ready for everybody else that was going to come over to see my brother and the way he died. My father looked out the windows and looked down into his hands. My mother sat down in chairs and touched her hair and wiped her eyes. My sister played with a doll that was supposed to make my brother alive again but it never did.

The whole time we stayed inside there there were people that came over to our house and up to our windows and looked at us inside. They brought over food in bowls and food on plates. They knocked on the windows and knocked on the doors and they waited there. They called us by our names but we never did say anything back to them. We couldn't let any of them come inside yet.

They left food on the windowsill and my mother would open the window far enough up to slide the food inside our house and us. They left more food outside the doors or on the porch and we would wait for them to leave before we brought the food inside to eat it. They would always look back at our house before they got into their cars and drove away from our house and our family and us. They were trying to see what we looked like and did and the way that we lived there after my brother died.

We lived inside our house and ourselves. We did not talk to

each other even though my mother would talk to herself. We got my brother and everything else in our family and house ready for everybody else to come over and inside and see it. People drove over from Sweetwater and Chico and Riverland and they parked their cars all up and down the road in front of our house and in our front yard. They drove in from Killeen and Overton and came inside our house to see my brother and us. They drove up from Tyler and Sugar Land and Old Dime Box and everybody wanted to talk about my brother and the way that we laid him down in his casket.

This lady from Amarillo talked about the dead people that we shared in our family—my brother and her sister. This man from Hull Lake told me that we die in families so that some-body remembers us and can tell other people about it. This man from Brownland told my sister and me that neither one of us was the dead one so we shouldn't cry anymore. This lady from Kossetown told us that we can't get away from our family or dying but that my mother and father would get another brother for us.

But everybody also stopped talking to us and looking at my brother and they all left my brother and us and our family and house. My father told us that my brother gone was enough for the rest of us to gather ourselves and our stuff up and leave that place too. We couldn't stay in our house or Mineola anymore. My brother was dead and we couldn't live there either.

My Doll-Family, My People-Family, the Sun Outside, My Little Brother's Insides, the Big-People, and How They Could Have Made Me Another One of My Little Brother

My doll-family plays better at family than my people one does. My Poppa-doll got lost somewhere but Momma told me it was okay for me to make me another Poppa-doll out of string-clothes and buttons and him all kept together with popsicle sticks.

The doll of my little brother got left out under the sun one day once and the yellow-fever colored my little brother in sun-colored. We had to take my little brother to see big-people where they put stuff inside his mouth and touched on how bright was the color of his forehead. There was the poke-poke lady with all her more fingers. There was the fold-handed man that threw drops of water all around the room but that never made it rain outside.

One more way they didn't make up to make him not as sun-hot as he was was ice cubes inside his diapers. One more way was saying baby and in and air and out from my mouth on him. One more way was coloring his skin back in skin-colored with my crayons. One more way was hanging his baby clothes up on tree-arms but that was only to be inside the shade.

The sun-color got too bright and too inside under my little brother's skin until it burned his insides out inside his crib. My little brother lived with me and my doll-family after he burned up inside and big-people came over to see how he did it. Big-people carried food over but we didn't even feed any of it to my little brother. The rest of us ate all of it even though we were all already alive. One man had tree-arms that carried a treeful of red apples and green apples and that kept anyone else from catching any yellow-fever from my little brother.

One more man pushed a button that made light flash that burned your eyes up but did not make it so hot as to burn us up inside. The light flashing made looking-pictures of my little brother on Momma's lap and one more way to make babies go away to alive. That man blew on the looking-pictures of my little brother until he was out of breath and which but that just left my little brother all small and flat.

My little brother was even littler when he was dead. But more and more big-people came over to our house and one more man had more ways than me to keep my little brother alive. That man wore a burnt-colored knee-coat that was still warm. You could see how hot it was in his hot-colored face and the way he blew his cheeks out to get the hot part out of him. Momma told me that dead people was all that that man did but that that man wasn't going to take my little brother away from us. We were going to take my little brother away with us. That man was just supposed to get him ready to go.

He undressed the clothes even though my little brother was already cold. But clothes can't be alive anyway and that man didn't keep going when he got down to my little brother's skin. That man took up a bucket of rain water and squeeze-clouds that he carried down with him out of the sky. That man squeezed the squeeze-clouds of rain water down over my little brother so it would drown him in the swallow of water and smoke the fire out that burned his insides up. He dried my little brother down inside a towel like the one they wrapped him up in to bring him home in after he was born. That man unwrapped the towel from my little brother and rained handfuls of rain water up over his head and down over his neck and out the ends of his hair. We combed it out and it looked nice. That man smelled his nose down into the neck and shoulder and snuffled my little brother. That man touched my little brother's eyelids down with his finger and thumb like Poppa would pull the window-cover down before he would put us down for sleep. But how was my little brother going to see us anymore when his eyes were closed?

That man stuffed cotton balls and worded-paper inside my little brother's mouth so he could see how to talk. That man got out the needle and thread and asked me how my little brother smiled. He threaded the thread through the needle and the needle and thread into and out of his lips so it could not be told. He got a moon-knife out of his night-bag and cut cuts inside both the elbows and the knees both. He pushed tubes into my little brother but we didn't feed him any food through them. The squeeze-pump sucked and pulled. It spit and pushed the blood. The tubes he looped into my little brother were outside-veins for the clear-blood that flooded the burned and dead-blood out from my little brother.

That man let me touch where my little brother should have started up again but my hand never breathed up or down on him. We hit and pushed my little brother on his rib bones but that didn't start his heart beating up or down again either. That just made my little brother go all see-through and angel-colored so we stopped squeezing the squeeze-pump and pulled the tubes out and stopped the holes up.

We colored his skin back in skin-colored with paint brushes from that man's night-bag. We painted his face and neck and hands back on him but it did not look real or alive enough even when it didn't even have to be pretty. That man told me let's dress him up nice so we put dress-up clothes on him but my little brother still didn't get up and live.

Our House in Mineola

The men went from living room to bedroom and bedroom and bathroom to kitchen. The men went into and out of the rooms and into and out of our house. The men went back and forth between our house and their truck. They got the couch up between two of them and carried it out. One of them took the cushions. Another one of them carried a chair. Another one of them carried another chair. Their arms and the other parts of them were all large. They made the doorways small with themselves and the furniture they carried out of the rooms, away down the hallway, and out of our house—table, lamp, table and chairs, dresser and dresser, bed and bed and bed.

These and the even bigger things they carried out across the front yard—ice box, bathtub, bathroom sink, kitchen sink, the kitchen table and chairs. They carried out boxes full of other stuff and carried other stuff out that did not fit into boxes. They rolled the carpet up and rolled the carpet up and folded it over their shoulders and shouldered it up into the truck. They pulled the cupboards from the kitchen walls down. The floors they pulled up—all the tile and board.

They took the windows out of the walls and took the way we

looked out of the windows away with them when they did that. They took the doors off the hinges and banged them shut inside the walls of their truck so that those closed doors left us outside but also opened the rest of America up for us.

The men pulled the stoop away from the front door and took that away with them too. All that stuff wasn't ours anymore and their truck was packed. The men climbed up into the truck and into the truck and into the truck. They sat down in the chairs at the kitchen table and among themselves and all the insides of our house that they had carried out. The last one of them pulled down on the rope that rolled the truck's rolling back door closed. He climbed up through the truck driver's front door and drove the truck and all our stuff that was inside the truck away from our house in Mineola to somewhere else in America.

My mother and father and brother and sister along with the other and smaller things that we had left were all that we had left of us in that house of our family and stuff. My mother and father packed the suitcases, boxes, and crates up with the rest of the stuff that was still ours. My mother and father packed my brother up in his casket and packed his casket up in the trunk. My mother and father carried everything else out to the car and packed it up too. My mother and father packed my sister and me up with the rest of the stuff that we had left and we left too.

The Baby-Sized Hole Inside the Ground and Dirt-World and the Toy Box with My Little Brother Inside It

They dug the baby-sized hole deep enough for any of the big-people to go down into it. One man pounded stab-holes with the bone-stick he pulled out of his shoulder and back and swung down out of his arm and into the ground and dirt-world. One more man did it with a big-spoon he dug out of the hole and bone of his leg and foot. They dug all the way down into the hole until we couldn't see them anymore but for their hands and arms and dirt and spoons and bones and sticks. But they didn't make the hole go all the way through. Neither one of them dug the baby-sized hole deep enough or far enough away or down enough under for my little brother.

But they could both go all the way down inside the hole and still be alive when they climbed back up and crawled back out of it. They were both too big to die and lay down inside the hole. But they pounded the nails down into the top side of the toy box so my little brother couldn't get out of it and they tied him up inside it with ropes too. They swung my little brother up over the hole with the ropes and they knocked the toy box back and forth against the side-walls all the way down to the bottom where the hole stopped.

But they didn't cover my little brother up with anything so he could stay warm and go away to sleep. They left the hole open so we could throw dirt on top of him but none of us were going to do it. They left the ropes with him for him to crawl with back out but we had to go and pull him back out of the ground and dirt-world with our hands and arms and backs and ropes. The toy box hit and knocked back and forth against the side-walls and the dirt and rocks all fell down under my little brother and started filling his baby-sized hole back up. We got the toy box out and knocked on its sides and listened for noises but my little brother was quiet inside. We unpounded the nails from the top side of the toy box and pulled it open and looked inside but my little brother was still inside there and he was still dead.

The pile of dirt and rocks by the side of the hole wasn't high enough and far enough away or up for him to climb on up into the sky and cloud. But we pushed the dirt and rocks back down into the hole and filled it back up with our hands and bones and shoes and hot and string and down and sun and burn and hills and ways and years and names and big and in and dolls and blood and dead and we kept my little brother up above the ground and dirt-world and with us.

Mineola to Birthrock

We drove away from our house and away down the road. We drove past some other houses that were all broken at the walls and didn't have any families living in them anymore. They had broken windows and broken doors. They had broken cars in the front yards that didn't have any tires on them so that those people that had lived there never left but stayed there and died.

We drove all the way out to the far part of Mineola where there were houses that had people and families that were still living in them. We stopped and got out of our car and walked up to this one house and looked in the windows but they were only old people that lived there and they didn't have any babies left in their family anymore so we didn't even knock. We needed to find a house with a family that was going to have a baby in it.

We knocked on doors and looked in windows until this other family that needed a baby came up to their door and answered us. Their faces were the only things we could see through their screen door—their mother and father, their brother and sister, and the way they looked like a family in there. Their family stood there behind their screen door and in their doorway and inside their house and with all their stuff. Their father pulled their brother and sister in close to him and his leg and hip and their mother stood next to him too.

Our family stood there in the same way but outside their house and on their porch and without anything with us but us. My father asked their family if they were going to have a baby in it and their father nodded that they were and their mother held the bottom of her stomach up with her hands. My father asked them to stay there and wait there and we went back to our car and opened the trunk up. My father got my brother's cradle out and my mother got my brother and the other baby stuff out. My mother gave my sister and me the small blankets and the little pillows, the stuffed animals and the other baby toys, and we all carried all that baby stuff back up to that family and their house and stood there on their porch with it.

My mother cradled my brother in the blanket in her arms and touched her hand over the blanket and my brother even though he wasn't crying or moving his arms and hands or even doing anything anymore. My mother kept my brother with her inside herself and in her arms. My mother wouldn't let anybody else hold my brother even when their mother talked like a baby talks and held her arms out for him. Their mother said that she wanted to practice with him some but my mother said the baby might break and she wouldn't let go of him. Their family's baby wasn't born yet and their mother cradling my brother in her arms might have killed the baby inside her stomach. Nobody else was supposed to touch my brother anymore or somebody else besides him might die in some other family or house.

The thing that killed my brother was that the cradle didn't have anymore baby years left in it. My mother didn't have anymore baby years left in her arms anymore either. My sister and me had already lived them all up and the other baby stuff didn't have enough baby years left in any of it to keep my brother alive. My brother's cradle was probably going to kill their family's baby too but they could not have known that yet.

They got my brother's cradle and other baby stuff and we got away from there. We walked away from them and back to our car so we could be a family again. My father opened the trunk up and my mother laid my brother down in his casket and closed its top and closed the trunk. The casket was the only other baby place that we had left for my brother after my mother wasn't holding him in her arms anymore. The rest of our family got back inside our car and closed the doors. Their family walked down off their porch and into the driveway so they could watch us go. Their family was a family there and then and we were going to be a family somewhere else. We drove away from them and they waved at us from their driveway and we waved back through our car windows.

They got my brother's cradle and other baby stuff and we got out of Mineola. The only baby thing we kept with us was my brother. We stayed a family that way. We drove away from Mineola and toward Birthrock—away from where my brother was alive once and died there and toward the miles and the everything else that was going to happen to us everywhere else we went.

We traded my brother's life away to that other family when we traded my brother's cradle and other baby stuff away to them. My brother and the baby he was going to be were going to grow up with some other family somewhere else. We got the life of my brother that we didn't leave buried in Mineola. That was why we were going to see my brother in so many other babies and other families and other places. My brother was going to be alive in Campbell Station and in Far Town and in other places that we went away to on our way to Bompa's house in Gaylord.

Our House-Car, Bompa's House, Going to Heaven, and When We Could Start Living Again

We drove our house-car over the road over and over until the tires got too hot and they colored the road in burnt-colored. But we weren't going to burn up inside our house-car or us. We rolled the windows all the way down so the wind could blow through the insides of our house-car and us and push the sun off from our faces and arms so we didn't burn up like my little brother did before he died.

We drove our house-car down into road-holes and rolled up out of them farther down the road. We hit little hills with our house-car and it lifted us up into the air until we weren't touching the ground or road-world anymore. We were going to Heaven.

Our whole people-family was going to start living again as soon as we got to Bompa's house in our house-car. Bompa wasn't going to let anybody else die after we got there. Bompa was going to have bedrooms for everybody to sleep inside them so we could all get up and live inside his house. There was going to be a living room that was big enough for us to all live together with my whole people-family and my little brother alive inside it too.

But we weren't living anywhere anymore. We kept leaving everywhere we went. We couldn't stop and live anywhere until we got to Bompa's house with our house-car and us and with everybody alive. We drove and rolled and bounced up and down inside our house-car the whole way there. Momma's head would go up and down and Poppa's would too. My bigger brother would hold on to his stomach and my insides would shake when they bounced up and fell down and they were empty inside them. You could hear the way my little brother would roll against the sides of the toy box and inside the trunk and you could feel it inside your own insides too.

Birthrock to Stringtown

My mother looked back and forth on both sides of the street for this other lady that we were looking for in Birthrock. My father leaned forward over the steering wheel so he could see her before we got up to where she was. That other lady saw our car and us looking for her and waved us over to her. She came over to our car and us to see if it was us and my mother handed her her necklaces and other dress-up stuff out the window. The only thing that my mother wouldn't give that other lady was the one last ring off her ring finger. My mother said that she was still going to wear it for as far away and long as they were married.

That other lady put the earrings in her earlobes, the other finger rings on her ring fingers, a necklace around her neck, and all of it went together. My mother told her that she didn't have anywhere to wear her necklaces or any of her other dress-up stuff anymore. That other lady asked us where we were going and my father said that we didn't know how much farther away we could get. That other lady looked inside our car and in at each of our faces. You could see by the way she looked in at us that she could see what had happened to us.

That other lady looked away toward the road and the way we were going to go away from her and there. She looked back at us again and said that she wanted to see what she looked like. She crouched down to look at herself in the side mirror on my mother's side door. She turned and looked in through the windows and inside our car at my mother and took my mother's looks away from her. My father looked past my mother to that other lady wearing all my mother's dress-up stuff. My mother looked at my father and farther away.

That other lady got my mother's dress-up stuff and looks. She looked at us and looked away again and then walked away too. We watched that other lady walk away from us through the car windows until we couldn't see her anymore and then we went away again too. My mother's necklaces and other dress-up stuff along with everybody's looks got us from Birthrock to Stringtown and you could see the way we all started to get so far away from each other. We sat in the far corners of the seats and leaned our shoulders up against the windows and doors. We drove away and looked out the windows for miles. My father used the side door and rearview mirrors to see what was behind us but we all knew what it was without looking back there.

Some More Ways Dolls Keep People Alive, the Way You Go Away from Doll to People and Bigger, and the Big-People We Were Going to Grow Up into and Live Them

Momma threw the baby away. Momma wrapped the baby up inside napkins and buried him down inside the trash. But the napkins didn't keep the baby warm enough and clumps of him got sticky inside the trash and cold. But we didn't throw my little brother away even when he got sticky inside his crib and cold. But Momma's baby-clumps weren't enough baby even when they were the color of anybody's insides and Momma's and blood.

Big-people make babies too small and die too soon. Doll-people make babies too. But doll-people and their babies might either be quiet or dead after they go alive. My little brother was too small to keep him alive even when the doll of him was doll-alive. You die when you don't get big enough to be one of the big-people or when you're doll and don't get people enough and then big. My people-me and doll-me were neither one of us big enough yet then. My bigger brother was bigger then than me but he still wasn't big enough to be one of the big-people or stay alive either.

Me and my bigger brother could have died like my little brother did. But my dolls of us kept both of us both people-alive. We played the dolls of us inside the car-shade so we didn't burn up inside the car-sun through the house-car window. We fed the dolls of us doll-food and put their doll-heads inside our mouths so we could breathe. We slept the dolls of us down on the place where your arm is supposed to rest and we woke them up so they would keep living with us.

My little brother was already dead and broken and the doll of him was too hot to be doll-alive. The sun followed my dolls and us inside our house-car to burn us all up. We tried to drive away from the sun to alive but it still burned the doll of my little brother up through the back window of the house-car. We still played family with the doll of him but he burned our hands up when we played with him too.

My people-family wasn't all alive and people-families need people. People-families need a Bompa to go away to and they need anybody else that's older and bigger or dead. But a people-family doesn't only need people inside it. We needed somewhere to live together too. We needed beds and rooms and the insides of our people-house and a new people-house to live inside it or somewhere to sleep or food and eat. But sometimes a people-family has something more to it or inside it or holding it together and the more can be glue and string or roads or dolls and babies or my little brother and the insides of people and blood. But sometimes a people-family is also missing something from inside it and it was the alive part of my little brother that was missing from inside us and we missed him too.

Momma told me Bompa was inside my people-family and he wasn't missing anything from inside his house and my little brother was going to be alive when we got there. We also had my doll-house inside the house-car with us but Momma wouldn't let me get it out until we got to Bompa's house. My doll-house was going to make Bompa's house a people-house where we could live inside it and there would be more rooms for my little brother and us that were bigger enough so we didn't have to leave it too.

My doll-house had doors that closed so people couldn't leave and sheets over the windows so the sun couldn't get inside it and my doll-people or us and burn anything up. My doll-house had beds and tables inside the bedrooms and kitchen so we could sleep and eat again when we got to Bompa's house. It had lights to see and windows so we could see outside and doors so we could leave again and go home then.

But my doll-people were too big to live inside my doll-house so me and my little and bigger brothers were going to grow up from little to bigger than any of the big-people. We were going to grow up out of the dolls of us and us and us and up into big-people and live them. Big-people get anything they want but it was going to take all of me and years for me to grow up to be that big and get the alive part of my little brother and everything else back.

Stringtown to Albion

My father stopped our car in front of this house that had toys in the front yard. There were toy cars and play trucks parked there for us to practice the ways to go away to other places with them. But the boy and girl that were playing in the front yard weren't playing to go away. They were practicing at house with a play fort that had play doors and real windows so when you went inside it everything was play and when you looked back outside it everything was real.

They sat down in play chairs at a play table so they could practice at mother and father and family and house so when they got to be a mother and a father with a family in a house none of them would die. They dressed up like a mother and father but they didn't play their family with a baby. They asked my sister and me to dress up and be their boy and girl but my mother and father wouldn't let us do it. My mother and father still needed us to be the kids for their family.

But the real mother and father of that boy and girl and family and house came out of their real house. My father gave them my sister's dollhouse and my mother gave them my sister's doll family. My father told my sister that she wasn't going to need her practice family or house things anymore since we weren't living in our house anymore. But that girl that got my sister's doll family and dollhouse already had a real family and a real house where they lived. That girl and her real family didn't look like they were going to leave that house or that anybody was going to die there either.

But my sister and me didn't have a real house or a real brother anymore. We didn't have a real family that had everybody living in it and we didn't have lots of other stuff either. My sister wasn't going to have her dollhouse and doll family to practice with anymore and everything else that happened to us after Stringtown was going to be real.

My sister tried to run away but she didn't get very far away before my mother caught up to her and walked her back into our family. My sister wasn't going to play family with her doll family anymore but all that doll stuff still got us from Stringtown to Albion.

We were going to go farther and farther away into the more real things in our family by driving away and by our need. We were going to trade everything else that we had left in our real family away and trade our real family away too. We were going to drive through towns and get through other places and things that happened all along the way. But we weren't going to get away from what happened to my brother and our family and we weren't going to be a family anymore after we got all the way there.

My Doll-Me, My People-Me, and the Way My Doll-Family Got Away

Poppa got my doll-house out of our house-car and put it down in front of this girl and her people-house. Momma took my doll-people away from me and put them down so me and that girl could play family with them. Momma told me to do the doll-people so that girl would know how to play the dolls into a family. But that girl already had a people-family with everybody living inside it and she didn't need to know how to do the doll-family or anything else.

But me and that girl walked the dolls with our hands and their feet and talked doll-talk with both their mouths and our mouths both. Doll-talk is small. But doll-talk still means something when you hear dolls say it. Doll-talk doesn't go away. It stays with you and keeps happening to you and you have to hear it out loud. But that girl told me to go away and she made the doll say it too. She walked my Momma-doll and my Poppa-doll away from me with her hands. But my dolls of me and my bigger brother stayed with me in my hands and my people-me told that girl to stop. Families go together.

So that girl took the dolls of me and my bigger and little brothers away from me and ran away too. But that's not how you're supposed to play with dolls or people that are real. You're supposed to play together until the dolls get old and break and die and you can't play with them anymore. You can't take everything doll away from me and make me go away too.

My people-me chased after that girl and everyone else ran after me and her too. She wasn't going to get the doll-me that was still me. But my people-me ran away until that girl fell up her people-house house-steps and all my dolls of us fell down out of her hands and arms. We weren't playing anymore but none of us died before she picked us all back up doll.

But that girl's hands and knees were blood-colored on the house-steps and missing the skin. She almost killed the dolls of us when she colored us in with her hands and knees and blood. But my people-me chased that girl inside her people-house and people-family and everybody else ran after us. But that girl got away from me with my doll-family. She was faster away than me inside her people-house and back outside she was farther away from me too.

Momma ran away after me and held on to me to hold the whole world still for me but everything else kept going farther away. My whole people-family had to go so fast away from there after that that that girl didn't keep us with her with the dolls there. Poppa drove the road-world away and Momma told me that we weren't going to die. But how far away could we go away and stay alive when my doll-family stayed there with that girl and her people-family? You have to keep your doll-you with you or there won't be a living-world for people or dolls or my little brother to live inside it anymore.

Albion to Hot Springs

We kept going until we ran out of gas and our car died out. My father got out and pushed. My mother reached over and steered. My sister and me walked behind our car and we pushed too. We rolled the car down off the road and into the truck stop and up to the truck stop's gas pumps. It was a truck stop but we stopped our car there too. There were lights on up on high poles and they stayed on the whole time we were there. There were big trucks that drove in under the light poles and drove over a metal rope that rang the night bell. They filled their gas tanks up with gas and their tires up with air. They drove their big trucks over to the side lot and parked them there. They let their air brakes out. They were going to stay there.

My father pumped the gas into the gas tank until it was full enough so we could keep going away from there. My mother washed the car-door windows so we could see more out to the side and my father washed the windshield so we could see farther away to Bompa's house.

The man inside the truck stop where you pay saw us looking in at him and waved us inside. He stood behind the countertop and had so many things around him that we didn't have. The man had short racks of sunglasses and hand games. There were long shelves with toy cars and car dolls, stuffed animals and talking animals and animals made out of rocks and shells. There were standing racks of license plates but none of them had our names on them. There were jars with lemon drops and jaw breakers and chocolate stars and rock candy. There were standing racks with maps.

The man asked us where we were going and my father told him that we didn't have any money. The man held out his hands and my father emptied his pockets out on top of the countertop—his pocketwatch and pocketknife, the key chain with the house keys, and some other things that he almost always kept with him whenever we went anywhere. My father told the man where we lived and gave him the house keys. My father told him that that pocketwatch and pocketknife were old but worked and the man let us eat there too. He sat us down in a booth and set full plates of food down in front of us too.

We ate everything he gave us to eat even though we didn't have anywhere to live anymore. That key chain of house keys traded our house in Mineola away for gas and food and miles so we would all keep going away and so that man's family could live inside it.

My father closed himself off from us when he traded his pocketknife away to that man and my father closed up inside himself too. My father trading that pocketwatch away traded the time he was going to spend with my sister and me away too. He didn't watch us as much anymore or really look at us in the same way either. My father looked off over our heads to where we were going away to but that was still farther away than he could see yet.

But that stuff from my father's pockets still got us from Albion to Hot Springs. We filled our gas tank up with gas and our stomachs up with food. We got back up on the highway and drove away until we were all the way out of Oklahoma and into Arkansas. It was easier for us to leave Albion and Oklahoma and everywhere else after we had fewer things and less stuff left. The other people that got our stuff stayed where they were at. Our stuff kept them there. They put their hands down in their pockets and watched us leave. My sister and me looked back out the back window and waved back at them until they were gone too.

How to Cut Dolls and People Out of Paper, Crayon-Faces, the String that Holds People Together, Holding Hands Together, and One More Way Any Family Can Break

Momma gave the dolls of us away and gave us away with them. Momma told me we're all still here aren't we and we all still were there. But Momma gave me paper for paper doll-people and me to play family with them but they weren't my real doll-family anymore.

Momma told me to make doll-people out of paper and folding and cutting and breathing and stretching the string of them out until it's a family that holds their hands together. But Momma's paper didn't have anything on it so you couldn't tell which ones of us the doll-people were or where they came from or how they lived.

We make each other up anyway. We are made up out of

other people and the living-world. But we also die from each other and go back down into the ground and dirt-world after we burn and poke and break and the people goes out of us.

But the folded-up paper made a skinny-world out of flat-people and we lived inside it. Momma gave me two knives with holes inside them that were sharp inside to cut with them. You push them together and pinch your skin up with them until you get holes inside your paper-skin and which but that fills up with blood so you can stay alive and the people doesn't leak out. But the paper doll-people got cuts with holes inside them and they didn't fill up with any blood. The holes filled up with air so the paper doll-people could breathe and go away to alive after they weren't folded up anymore.

But when you open them up and pull them away from each other then you've got a paper doll-family that holds hands and goes together. But the string of them was too long and far away so they were too many paper doll-people for my people-family and some of them had to go away.

But you don't know which ones of them are your people-family since a string of paper doll-people are all the same and not big or little or baby. But when you pull on both ends of the paper doll-people string then the string will break and you can tell which paper doll-people live inside your people-family and which ones of them were from somewhere else where we left them back there. But the string of paper doll-people doesn't always break into family. Sometimes you have to tear them off from one string and family and tape or glue them to another one.

Paper doll-people need their fingers and toes and faces colored in with crayons after you know you want to keep them. You make faces with eyes and ears and a nose and mouth so they can see and hear and smell and breathe and talk and eat and go away to people.

But crayons don't really make faces real. Crayons only make faces play. But my paper doll-people didn't fill up with air for breathing or grow up into any dolls that were bigger or people. My little brother was flat inside the toy box and trunk and couldn't sit up. My paper doll-people never got tall or wide or people enough to be alive either. But nothing happened to my people-family after my paper doll-people broke their hands and let go of each other.

But my paper doll-people flew away out the window and played going home. They weren't going away to Bompa's house with us anymore. They were going away to family somewhere else away from us. But that can happen to a people-family too. My little brother was broken off from us and the rest of us were almost broken too.

Hot Springs to North Little Rock

We drove through the wind and along the lake and over the hot water in the lake and into Hot Springs. There was steam coming up out of holes in the ground and there were hot people with sweat coming out of their skin. There were whole families of hot people. There were fathers that weren't wearing any shirts and mothers that wore blowing away hats and skirts. There were boys and girls that had clothes that were too small and wet and that didn't fit them.

My father stopped our car in the road and my mother got out of it. My mother took my suitcase out of the trunk and my clothes out of the suitcase and laid my clothes out in outfits on top of the trunk. The clothes were warm from the sun burning through the trunk and suitcase. But we left my brother in the trunk and in his casket even though he was hot from the sun and his fever that never went down.

This other mother walked up to us and told us that she needed clothes for her boy to wear until he grew up. This other mother touched my clothes down on the trunk and my mother said that he looked like the right size of me. My mother and his mother made us take our clothes off in the road but they didn't have anything else for me to wear yet. That other boy put my clothes on and took my clothes off and folded them up into stacks and put them back into my suitcase.

Everybody looked at me and that other boy and that other boy started to look like me but smaller. My clothes were too big for him to wear but that other boy's mother traded us for them and the other baseball stuff that was too small for me too. That other boy was going to wear my clothes out and grow up into my life and them and play me. That other boy that got my clothes got my life. He was going to wear out those clothes that my brother was supposed to grow up into them.

My new life was going to be me growing up into the handed-down-to-me suit of clothes that was too big for me then and then into the too-big-for-me life that was mine then too. My life got bigger and older after that. But those clothes of mine, the baseball stuff that was too small for me, and the lives of my brother and me—all those things still got us from Hot Springs to North Little Rock and farther away from where my brother died. The clothes and the other smaller stuff got us closer to those other places where we sometimes found my brother alive.

Sometimes and in some places it was just some baby stuff that made my brother alive for us. Other times and some-where else it was my sister and what she did. But there were always going to be more places and more people with other babies that looked like my brother did before he died. There were going to be other families in other places where my brother could have lived after he couldn't live with us or in our family in Mineola anymore.

48

House-Cars, Car-People, the Safety-Bars that Saved Me and My Bigger Brother, Some More Ways We Got Some of Everything Back, and Why Everybody Needs to Stop and Rest or They Will Break

Poppa drove us going away from the sun so we didn't get any hotter than we were before we left for the alive part of my little brother. The road-world breathed through our house-car until we drove into the burnt-colored sky at nighttime with everybody that was dead. But my bigger brother told me there were going to be more hot things to burn us up the farther we drove away into where the sun burns in the field.

But we weren't there yet then. We were still little and going and living inside our house-car where my little brother's room was inside the trunk where he slept inside the toy box for a crib. He shared his room with Poppa's tools and one more tire for when another one of the tires rolls out of breath. But we didn't have one more of my little brother to put anymore air inside him so don't let him get worn out or holes so the people leaks out of him or the skin wears down to too thin and goes to see-through angel-skin.

But Poppa told me we were going to get new lives when we got up to Bompa's house and Heaven. But Poppa stepped down hard on the brake and stopped the moving road-world. My little brother was already broken and sometimes we had to stop and rest or we'd break too. But when you stop and rest then everybody else inside the moving road-world keeps going past you and you might die where you stopped at.

Me and my bigger brother were living inside the backseat-room of our house-car all the daytime but we slept on top of the rooftop at nighttime. We didn't want to burn up inside the house-car with the night-sun on inside it at nighttime. The night-sun touches on you hot and sleepy when you look up into it too spotty and blind. We didn't want Momma and Poppa to leave us there to sleep and die under it like my little brother did outside our house and inside him.

But me and my bigger brother were too big for the safety-bars on top of the rooftop to save us. We had had safety-bars for our cribs and beds from when we were even smaller little-people and still lived at home. My little brother had had safety-bars for his baby crib too but they didn't save him. Me and my bigger brother were still alive but the safety-bars kept us from rolling over and falling out of our sleeping-world and down on to the ground and dirt-world.

But you could see Momma and Poppa sleeping inside our house-car where they moved back and forth on each other and hot. Momma and Poppa stopped when they started to sweat too hot so they wouldn't burn up inside them like my little brother did. Momma and Poppa rolled the windows down and opened the doors up and pushed all the hot out of our house-car and the nighttime got colored in more burnt-colored.

Momma and Poppa slept inside the frontseat-room and backseat-room of our house-car and they did it with the doors open so they could sleep as far away out into the nighttime as they needed to to go away to sleep. Me and my bigger brother got up and got down off the rooftop of our house-car and out into the nighttime.

Everybody else sleeps and dies at nighttime. There are dead people inside house-cars and under them too. There are dead people inside the places where you stop at. There are dead people under the tables where you eat and down on the sidewalks and up inside the house where you can rest until you go away again. But nobody stays and lives inside that house. Everybody dies and rests and leaves there too.

Nobody could see us inside the dark. You can go out inside

the nighttime and take babies or anything else away with you when nobody sees you do it or told. Me and my bigger brother went away to where we could get into house-cars that had car-people in them and long trucks that were filled up with everything that comes out of a house so we could start living again when we got up to Bompa's house and Heaven. Car-people sleep with the windows open so you can go inside their house-car with your hands and arms and take anything back from them that was supposed to be yours when you went away from home. But sometimes car-people would sleepwalk and saw us so we almost got caught. But their eyes looked too sleepy and walked away from us or closed back up so they were blind and we got away.

Me and my bigger brother were too little for the big-people to see us anyway. We went away under the windows between the house-cars and went inside them so my little brother would have things to live with him when we got the alive part of him back. We took sunglasses that kept the sun out of our eyes so it didn't see inside us and burn us up. We got more folded-up paper that had lines and dots and names for places so we could find the way up to Bompa's house and Heaven. We got tools and napkins and string and shoes to make my doll-house and doll-family back up again. We got keys back so we could get back into my doll-house after we made it back up and get back inside our bigger house when we got up to

Bompa's house. We got food-bones and clothes and more string and sticky things and bottle caps and pop cans and baby shorts and baby-parts.

We buried everything we got back inside the trunk-room of our house-car and under my little brother inside the toy box. Me and my bigger brother closed my little brother's room down and went away inside the house where you can rest and washed our hands clean so nobody would catch us from touching on any of it.

North Little Rock to Campbell Station

My father needed to stop and sleep and my mother did too. It was this place where there were more sleeping people than us and everybody but my sister and me were doing it. There were people that slept in their cars—in the front seat or the back seat, leaning back or stretched out. There were people that slept in their trucks—up in the cab or out in the bed of it. There were people that slept in tents made out of blankets and other people that slept in tents that were really tents. There were even more people that were sleeping in sleeping bags under picnic tables and in the long grass and on the sidewalk.

There were other people that didn't have anything to sleep with but themselves at night. They grabbed their arms with their hands and held on to themselves that way. They laid down on their sides and pulled their knees up to their stomachs or hunched their shoulders and heads down into their knees and legs.

People woke up in the morning and let go or uncurled themselves but they were still sleeping people. They stood up and reached up. They folded up their blankets and folded up their tents. They rolled their sleeping bags up and tied them up with sleeping-bag string.

But there were more people that still needed sleep and we traded them our pillows, blankets, sheets, and the other stuff that helped us sleep. We got up and they slept more and that stuff got us from North Little Rock to Campbell Station.

We didn't sleep as much anymore after North Little Rock or for as far away into the night. We stayed up longer and drove farther away to sleep. We kept going away into the night until we got filled up with things that had already happened. My brother was still dead and we were still driving away from that. But the night gets filled up with other things that happen when you can't sleep. You think of them fast and they go through your head and into your life. Your mother and father are going to make another baby and your family is going to have another brother in it. You are going to play with your brother again but he is going to burn up again too. Your mother and father are going to go away without you with them anymore. Bompa isn't going to be there when you get there. Your sister is going to die and you are going to die too.

How You Get the Breath All the Way Down into Momma and the Baby Alive, How Poppa Laid the Babies Down to Sleep and Grow Up Inside Momma, and Why We Kept Waking Each Other Up

Poppa told Momma Momma's still pretty even when she doesn't wear any necklaces or anything else but clothes. But Momma told me she couldn't make a baby up again until her insides were alive again.

Babies don't get made or born with any clothes on them. But unless the baby is already alive then it might not grow up out of its clothes and die too soon. But Momma and Poppa made a baby out of skin and hair and talking and quiet. Momma and Poppa made a baby out of baby-talk and the quiet after babies stop talking and crying and die. Momma and Poppa made baby-noises so this new little brother baby they were going to make up and my little brother wouldn't die again.

Momma and Poppa rubbed and touched and kicked and hands and arms and legs and feet. Momma and Poppa yelled and stopped and you get more baby that way. Poppa breathed hard into Momma's mouth to get the breath all the way down into Momma and the baby alive.

Poppa laid the baby down to sleep and grow up inside Momma. But Momma and Poppa didn't make their baby even big enough to live even when they were already big and alive. Poppa didn't keep rubbing the baby-egg until it was just warm but not burned up. Momma and Poppa stopped making the baby and went to sleep even though me and my bigger brother had to keep waking each other up to see if we were still alive.

Campbell Station to Biggerton

My father stopped our car but kept it going and we stayed inside it. We rolled the windows down and looked out of them until we saw this other mother that had kids with her but no purse. My mother waved this other mother over to us and handed her her purse out the window. My mother told her that her purse would look good with almost anything she had to wear and anywhere she went. That other mother traded us for my mother's purse along with every small thing left inside her purse—candy and mints, lipstick and other make-up, pencils and pens, and bunches of other stuff my mother almost always kept with her whenever we went anywhere.

But that other mother got more than my mother's purse and every small thing inside it. She also got the looks that my mother would have made up with the make-up. We could see in through my mother's face and eyes to where there were more and other things missing from inside her that she could not cover up anymore. We couldn't see these more and other things inside her but we could see that they weren't there and we could still feel them too. They can be talking or looking and seeing or feeling or eating and other things anybody needs inside them but my mother didn't have them inside her anymore. We didn't have these things in between my mother and the rest of us in our family anymore either.

My brother wasn't alive anymore but we looked for him when we heard a baby cry or a baby rattle rattle or saw a baby carriage going down the street. My mother would touch her shoulder to hitch her purse strap up higher on her shoulder or touch as far down as her hip for her purse but it wasn't there anymore either. My mother would touch at her pockets or stomach or throat or hair or arms and hands together.

But my mother's purse along with every small thing inside her purse and the more and other insides that were inside her still got us from Campbell Station to Biggerton. We got farther away by trading everything else we had left with us or inside us away to everybody else that lived in everywhere we went. We were going to empty everything out of our family and empty everything out of everybody in our family. We got emptier the farther away that we went away together. We drove away past empty places—ditches along the side of the road, houses without any windows or doors, barns without roofs, fields without any trees or anything else growing up in them. We got out to where my mother and father and brother and sister and me only had miles and towns and the everywhere that we went away to together inside us. It was this emptiness and distance in between these places and us that held our family together in America.

How to Make a Doll-Baby Out of String, Baby Clothes, Shoe Parts, Buttons, Stones, Balloons, a Hat, Glue, Crayons, a Needle and Thread, and Two People Too

Doll-babies aren't strong enough to pick anything up when their fingers are made up from string. Doll-babies can't stand up either when their legs are string-legs. But people-babies can't stand up either. People-babies fall down when you let go of their fingers and hands or arms. It's their knees and hips that make you need both pins and sticks. Popsicle sticks or sticks that grow up out of trees are hard and bone enough to make the legs of doll-babies stand up under them but then their legs don't bend and break at the knees.

A shoe tongue should be too big for the baby's mouth so the baby will grow up into it and talk. Shoe heels make feet that can stand up and live. But stones can also make doll-babies stand up when stones grow up out of the ground where we stand on top of it. But Momma wouldn't let me glue or feed any stones to my little brother. But stones also look out for eyes. Buttons can look out for eyes too. But buttons are more for when the babies get born. But when a button has a string tied on to it then you can pull up the string until it breaks and the baby goes alive.

But the baby that Momma and Poppa are making up isn't big enough yet for it to live outside Momma's stomach and hole. But the baby can't be a girl. We already have one of me with us. We need an alive one of my little brother to live with us.

It takes two people to make a baby up and me and my bigger brother were going to make a baby up out of baby-stuff. The first baby-part for another doll of my little brother was a baby shirt that we filled up with baby socks and baby shoes. We used chicken bones for rib bones and blew a balloon up inside him to keep air inside him so he could breathe again. We made him eat up candy hearts for a people-heart and we ate some up too. We tied string up for veins and tied shoelaces together for the other stomach guts. We stuffed more clothes inside him so he wasn't so skinny and so he would start out bigger than he was when he was born the first time. We tied the neck hole and the arm holes up so my little brother's insides wouldn't come out again.

Momma helped us make the body of the doll-baby go

together. Momma got a needle and thread out and poked them into and out of the baby shirt and some baby pants so they would go together and my little brother would grow up and stand up and walk. But the doll of my little brother didn't have any hands or feet on his arms and legs.

But we still needed to hold on to my little brother with our hands and our family. We needed a head to make him up into a baby that we could play with him too. We did it with a baby hat from before when my little brother was alive but it didn't keep the sun out of his mouth. But Momma poked the needle and thread into and out of the hat and his shoulders and him so he would have a neck and a head.

But my little brother still needed his face so we colored his face in skin-colored with crayons and also gave him lips and ears and a nose. But we colored too many people-years in on his forehead. But we smoothed the wrinkles out inside his skin so he wouldn't be an old baby already and die too soon. We glued buttons on his face for his eyes so he could see but you can't let the glue go inside the eyeholes or it makes the baby's eyes go milky and blind.

We took my little brother and put him up under Momma's dress. We tied my little brother up to Momma's leg with string. We pulled on the string until it broke and Momma yelled and my little brother went away to doll-alive. It isn't a family when you don't have everybody living inside it anymore.

Biggerton to Glenallen

We drove past families in their cars and in their front yards. We drove past families going into stores and coming out of houses. We drove past families going into places to eat and families that were eating at picnic tables outside. There were families that had some old people or a baby in them and families that didn't have any of them.

We had my brother with us but he wasn't in our family anymore. But a family needs people in it to keep going or it stops being a family. We kept going and driving our family away from home and stopped at this place that had this other family stopped there. They wanted to take my sister and me away from our family and keep us for their family but my mother and father weren't going to trade us or any other people away to them.

My mother told them that we had other family to stay with if we could get there and my father asked them if there was anything they needed for their family—toys or shoes or tools, a wedding dress or a wedding ring. But they didn't say that they needed any of those things or anything else that holds or keeps a family together. They just looked back at us and shook their heads back and forth and if you looked at them and then looked back at us then they looked like they already had everything that you need to be a family.

But we were still able to trade them a locket and chain that my sister was wearing around her neck and that was from a smaller and older part of our family and us. It had a picture of my sister inside it from when she was a baby and sick and that had been cut out of a bigger picture that had more of our older family in it.

My mother was holding my sister in her arms in the bigger picture but the cutout picture of her was just her by herself and without any family with her. So my mother picked the locket and chain up off my sister's neck and chest and lifted it up over her head and laid it back down over that other girl's head and around her neck so it rested against her chest. That other girl opened the locket up and took the picture of my sister out of it. She put my sister's picture away in her pocket and kept the way my sister almost died with her when she did that. That other girl closed the locket back up and she didn't put anything in it so nothing bad would happen to her or her family.

That locket and chain that that other girl got from us got us from Biggerton to Glenallen in Missouri. My sister got to keep living with us in our family and we kept going farther away into our family the whole way to Bompa's house.

How to Make a Baby Up, How to Make Me Up into a Momma, and How Many People Any People-Family Needs to Have Living Inside It

Momma told us we couldn't play inside the toy box and trunk. But we played with the doll of my little brother so we didn't need the dead one of him anyway. But me and my bigger brother were going to make a new doll-baby up out of us like Momma and Poppa were making a new baby up too.

Me and my bigger brother put the baby-things inside the hole inside me and under my clothes to make a baby up and make me up into a Momma too. We rubbed baby shoes on my stomach. We ate baby food with our hands and wore baby clothes on small parts of us. We made Momma and Poppa hold us up on their shoulders and we pulled on our toes and sucked on our thumbs. We talked baby-talk and crawled around on the ground and pulled at their pant legs. We touched on hands and arms. We rubbed legs and feet and pushed on each other breathing hard. We yelled and stopped.

We held my hands over my nose and mouth to hold my breath inside me and my stomach out. We pushed my stomach out from behind me to make me up into more baby and bigger out.

We cut me and my clothes open to get the baby out of me and blood. But our baby only came out doll-baby. It wasn't crying or talking or eating and angel or folded up and paper or big enough either. It wasn't alive or living. Our doll-baby was bloody with my Momma and string.

But we hit the doll-baby and pulled on the string until it went from doll-alive to people and started living inside my people-family with us. The doll of my little brother going away to doll-alive helped Momma and Poppa make up the new little brother baby that they were making up for my people-family. Momma got bigger out and more baby. But we couldn't cut the baby out of Momma until it got up to big enough inside her but that was going to be a big ways away from where we were.

But Momma and Poppa yelled at me and my bigger brother when we cut my Momma-me out of my clothes and cut the baby out of me and blood. My bigger brother cut my dress open on my stomach and hole and all the way down me to blood. But Momma told me we can't go anywhere with you wearing that. But Momma and Poppa weren't going to leave me there or dead when they didn't leave my little brother anywhere else or dead either.

Momma undressed my clothes and Poppa touched the blood off my skin even when it never went away to angel-colored like my little brother's did. He stopped the blood and people from going out of me to dead and Momma dressed me back up into bigger clothes so we could go away to a bigger people-family than we were before we left home. Momma and Poppa needed all of us all alive for us to get back to the bigger people-family they had of us and that we were going to make up again out of each other and other people in Heaven and family and blood.

Glenallen to Anna

My father didn't have any money left in his wallet or pockets. He touched at all his pockets and he showed the men standing at the countertop that there wasn't any change money left in the change pocket or any paper money left in the long bill-folding part of his wallet either. There were just the cards with the names of other people and other places on them and there were the pictures of us from when our whole family was alive and together. Those men took my father's wallet and took all the stuff inside the wallet out of it. They took the cards out and spread them out on top of the countertop and they took the pictures of us out and tacked them up on a wallboard that made it look like we were their family.

My father backed away from the countertop and walked away from those men. We got back inside our car and closed our car doors. My father drove our family away from those men there but we weren't going to go away to any of those other places on those cards or see any of those other people anymore. There were cards for where to buy tires and fix the car or go to the doctor. There was this one card with the name of somebody that could build us a new house and one with somebody else that could paint the house and one more with somebody else that could lay the carpet down inside the house. There was this one card with the name of somebody that could make tables and chairs for the rooms of the house and there was one more with somebody that could sell the house when we were done living in it. But we weren't going home or for help and none of those things were really going to happen anymore.

My father's wallet, all those names of people and places on those cards, and all those family pictures of us got us all the way from Glenallen to Anna and we kept going away. My father traded our family away from us when he traded those family pictures of us away from us for miles. But those men probably tore the family pictures of us up and threw us away after we got away from them. That made us go farther away from them and each other and our family got farther away too.

Looking, Looking-Pictures, the People Inside Momma, the Shape of the Baby, and Looking Inside Momma's Stomach and Hole

My bigger brother told me he could still see me and Momma and Poppa told me they could still see me too. But how could my bigger brother or anybody else see me anymore after that girl looked at me and then kept the looking-picture of me with her?

Even big-people looked at us and then looked away from us. We didn't have enough people inside our people-family for them to see us.

But Poppa told us to look at Momma and Momma was already showing us the baby. But even when Momma undressed her dress then you could only see the outside of her stomach over the baby and not the baby inside her. We poked and rubbed Momma's stomach and hole and Momma rounded her hands around the shape of the baby and held her stomach up. Momma undressed her underwear and pulled her hair back and showed me her hole where the baby was going to come out of it. My bigger brother and Poppa couldn't look but it was too far away up there and dark for me to see the baby anyway. But Momma was hotter in there too and fire-colored. But don't let Momma's insides burn up like my little brother's did or burn up my new little brother baby on the way out either.

Poppa touched on Momma's stomach and Poppa told Momma you could see how this baby was going to be so big. But what was going to happen to the new growing baby of my little brother after he got too big to live inside Momma's stomach anymore and he had to come out of Momma's hole and live outside her too soon? But where did the baby of me or my bigger brother go away to after we got bigger and older and farther away than when we were baby? How do you know when you get up to bigger and that that is the people-you you are supposed to grow up into and to go away then and live them?

But Momma knew how to make babies up inside her and make them go alive outside her too. Momma had done it before with me and my bigger brother and she just needed this one of my little brother up inside her so my little brother could live with us inside our people-family again.

Anna to Henderson

My guns went off and people fell down. Birds dropped out of the trees or the bullets missed them and they flew away to live up into the sky. The stars got shot out at night. Street lights and house lights and car lights went out too. Windows broke. Tires blew out. My guns, holster belt, and bullets were only supposed to be for play but they also made all those things really happen.

Everything that happened after Anna was going to be even more real than everything that happened after we traded my sister's practice family away. We weren't ever going to get everything we traded away back. We were going to get other things in other places but nothing was ever the same thing. We were going to have a new baby living in our family but my brother wasn't ever going to be living again. We were going to have to live with my brother with us even though he was dead.

But it wasn't just my brother that was going to be dead anymore. There were going to be more and more dead people after that other boy got my guns, holster belt, and bullets. There were going to be more cemeteries that we drove past along the road and almost all of them were going to have gates that were closed so nobody alive could go inside there and there were only dead people there. But there were some cemeteries where they opened the gates and let people that were alive come inside and have a funeral.

Somebody would drive the dead person inside first and then the other funeral cars would drive inside after them but real slow. They could have driven the dead person away from there but nobody else ever did. They would drive them up to the hole and then everybody would leave the dead person there and leave there. They would leave the cemetery without a grandmother or grandfather or granddaughter or grandson or son or daughter or mother or father or brother or sister or baby with them or in their family anymore. Nobody lives in cemeteries. You have to leave them before your life starts up again.

We started to leave Anna, Illinois but that other boy started shooting at our car and us as we drove away from there on our way to Henderson. That other boy chased us out to the end of his driveway with the guns out in his hands and shooting the whole way. My sister and me ducked below the back seat windows as we drove away but that other boy must have kept shooting at us and everybody else even after we got too far away from him for him to hit us or kill anybody else in our family. Other people were going to die and be dead everywhere else we went away to and we couldn't stop it.

One of the Holes that Goes Down into the Ground and Dirt-World and Away to My Little Brother, the Other Momma and Poppa that Climbed Us Up and Up Out of the Hole, and How Our Momma and Poppa Kept Us Inside Our Family

My bigger brother pushed me down into one of the holes inside the dirt-world that goes away to where my little brother is at and after it didn't kill me then my bigger brother jumped down into it after me. But we didn't go away to Heaven or die. But we couldn't climb up out of down where we were either. There weren't anymore ropes or big-people to climb us back up and up with them.

But my bigger brother told Momma and Poppa and Momma and Poppa and out so loud. But they couldn't hear us anywhere near where we were and nobody else probably heard us either. We stood up and jumped up and waved our arms up but nobody saw us and helped us.

Me and my bigger brother started digging the farther way down. The dirt was harder and colder the farther away we went away down into the ground and dirt-world and it kept falling back down around our feet and shoes and started to cover us up even when we weren't the dead ones.

The sun got so high up it burned me and my bigger brother up and went up to burnt-colored on the rocks and stones and dirt and mud and us. It dried and cracked us. We almost broke and hot and burned and died. But we threw the rocks and dirt and everything else up out of the ground and dirt-world and up into the living-world outside us where everybody else but us lived.

We kept going up to the side-walls of the hole to hold on to the rocks and dirt and hand-climb our way up and up but the side-walls fell down and covered our feet and shoes up and up. The more and more we climbed and climbed and up and up the more and more the rocks and dirt and rocks and dirt covered us up and covered us up. But we weren't dead and nobody else was throwing the rocks and dirt back down on top of us and into the hole or covering us up.

But there was a Momma and a Poppa that weren't our Momma and Poppa standing up over us over the hole so they could save us and climb us up and up and out of where. The Poppa of them climbed down into the ground and dirt-world to carry us up and out and up and out and into the hands of the Momma and into the hands of the Momma. The Momma and Poppa held on to us so hard so we didn't fall down into the hole and down into the ground and dirt-world to where my little brother was at and get us lost anywhere else or die.

The Momma and Poppa asked us whose little boy and little girl we were and where we lived but we didn't live anywhere then. The Momma and Poppa told us they wanted us to stay there and make a bigger people-family with them but they didn't have a baby or my little brother either. But the Momma and Poppa told us to go and took our hands away from us and wouldn't give them back. We pulled on them to stop them but our hands and arms almost broke off from us.

The Momma and Poppa pulled us up off the ground and out of the living-world where the wind wasn't blowing and the living-world wasn't breathing anymore. But my bigger brother told Momma and Poppa and Momma and Poppa out loud and more and more big-people grew up out of everything there was there. There were house-people and car-people and road-people and door-people and window-people and all of them were looking-people too. The looking-people told us whose little boy and little girl we were but we were only my me and his him. But my bigger brother told them they weren't our Momma and Poppa and our Momma and Poppa came back and got us.

But our Momma and Poppa told the other Momma and

Poppa we weren't theirs and where were their babies anyway. Our Momma and Poppa wouldn't take anything else for us or give us away to the other Momma and Poppa. Momma and Poppa were going to keep me and my bigger brother together with them for so far away that we were still living with my little brother with us.

Poppa told the other Momma and Poppa to go away and Momma told the looking-people they couldn't see us anymore. The other Momma and Poppa stopped talking and the looking-people went away back to their cars and houses and roads and windows and doors and nobody else would look at us anymore but us.

Henderson to Hendricksville

We stopped at the rest stop so my mother could change her clothes and wear her wedding dress the rest of the way into Henderson. My mother wore her wedding dress over her other clothes so it looked like she was going to get married again. But my mother and father didn't need to get married again. They were already a family with my sister and me with them.

My mother took her wedding dress off and pulled her marriage up over her other clothes and her head until it didn't look like she was going to get married again or anymore and she looked like my mother in our family again. My mother gave this other lady the wedding dress so she could wear it down over her underwear and get married in it too.

My mother and that other lady stood there and looked at the way the wedding dress hung down and fit. They took parts of the wedding dress and pulled them away from her body and pinched them together so that other lady and the man she was going to marry would stay together and married. There were other parts of the wedding dress where they cut holes in them and then covered them back up with lace so those married things wouldn't happen to them where they did to my mother and father and their marriage.

My mother took her wedding ring off her ring finger and that other lady pushed and pulled my mother's wedding ring on to and off of her ring finger to see whether she could wear it for her whole marriage. That was probably where the marriage for my mother and father started to stop.

That was also where my mother didn't look like she wanted any of that wedding and marriage stuff anymore but we stayed there for their wedding anyway. There were more people than us that came over there to see them get married. They came over there in wedding pairs and family groups— men and women together, men and women and their families, men and women and boys or girls or old people that didn't have a husband or wife with them anymore.

Nobody came over without anybody else with them but for the man that stood up and looked out at everybody there. He told that other lady and the other man that she married what they needed to say to each other so we could all hear it. The man that talked looked like the same man that looked out at us and talked while we all stood over the hole where we were supposed to bury my brother. But my mother and father didn't say anything back to that man and we took my brother back out of the hole.

Nobody has to die for there to be a wedding or a marriage. There are dead people that aren't there and nearly everybody else sits down. The two people that are going to get married walk down the middle of everybody else and they stand up sideways in front of them. My sister and me did the same walk but she carried the flowers and it was me that carried the rings out of our family and into the family that those two other people were going to make up. But they didn't keep my sister and me in their family. My mother and father still needed us in their family and those two other people that got married were going to get their boy and girl and baby from each other for their family someday and somewhere else.

Everybody stayed there until those two other people that got married got in their car and left. Everybody else probably went home but us. But we left too. My mother's wedding dress, wedding ring, and other wedding stuff got those two other people married and got us from Henderson to Hendricksville. My mother didn't have anything else left from her wedding anymore but my father and my mother didn't have anything else left from our family but my father and us.

My Little Brother and His Breath Inside the Toy Box, How We Played with the Doll and People of My Little Brother, and How Alive You Have to Be to Go Away

Momma and Poppa told us don't touch on my little brother so we wouldn't catch any of his dead and go away to where everybody's already got all their dead. Don't but my bigger brother told me me and him could go look inside the toy box and trunk for my little brother and play with him after Momma and Poppa went away into the nighttime to sleep. You can go away from Momma and Poppa when they aren't looking at you or anybody else and our house-car wasn't moving away to anywhere else.

We opened the trunk up and the burn made everything smell hot inside it. The breathing inside my little brother must have pushed up and down and out of him until it filled the toy box and trunk up with the hot and burn of my little brother. The hot from it burned up from the toy box and trunk and my little brother and it burned my and my bigger brother's faces up until we looked away from it.

My bigger brother unpounded the nails back out of the toy box with the back of the short tree-fork and pulled them out and pushed them into his mouth and teeth. My bigger brother opened the toy box up and more hot and smell burned up from my little brother. It looked like my little brother was smaller inside the toy box and older than when he was alive. My little brother's head and face were wrinkled down. My little brother was sucking his cheeks inside his mouth to breathe but he couldn't get anymore breath inside him. The hot and smell burned up out of his nose until me and my bigger brother couldn't breathe anymore either. We held our breath inside us with our fingers and hands.

But my bigger brother told me to put the trunk-gloves on and he did it too even when it wasn't cold anymore. But we did it to get my little brother up out of his dead and into people again. We bent my little brother up at the stomach and legs and sat him up against the toy box until it looked like my little brother was the doll of my little brother and we could fix him back up to doll or people enough to play with him again.

We pulled his cheeks back out with the finger-pinchers but they just made holes inside his face and didn't even breathe his cheeks back out. We opened his lips and mouth up with the short knife until he smiled. We unheld his arms from together with the small tooth-cutter. We made the tire-cross stand up behind him to hold his arms back out again but his arms didn't work enough to hug us or even hold on to anything else even when it looked like my little brother was trying to hold on to everything in my people-family and us.

We used all those tools up on my little brother but they didn't fix him enough up for him to go away to alive again. My little brother's clothes were the only things holding him together anymore. But we undressed the clothes off my little brother anyway. His skin was so loose as his clothes were but it was still holding him together too. My little brother's hair was longer from when he tried to grow up even when he was already dead. My little brother's fingernails and toenails were bigger and longer too. They grew up out of his fingers and toes but we still couldn't open my little brother up like we opened the toy box up. But we got my little brother up and dressed his clothes back up on him until they fit him to alive.

We shook my little brother but he still wouldn't wake up. He wouldn't crawl or walk either. My little brother wouldn't hold on to me or my bigger brother and we couldn't hold on to him too hard either or we might break him again.

We got the doll of my little brother out and played with him so we could make my little brother come back to alive with us.

We played with the doll of my little brother to get the play and dead and doll all the way out of him so he could go away to little-people and us and big-people with us.

My bigger brother took the worded-paper out of my little brother's mouth but my little brother didn't talk and say how hot or burned up he was inside him. But maybe my little brother wasn't big enough to put the words together when they were all said and balled up inside his mouth.

We drank him water and fed him food but he wouldn't swallow any of it. We touched on him with the alive we had left inside us even when we could have died from doing it too. We walked my little brother's legs around doll and people but they would only stop and fall down when me or my bigger brother stopped and let them go. We dropped the doll of my little brother inside the toy box and it died there too.

Momma and Poppa woke up and stood up out of our house-car. Momma and Poppa were babies and naked and yelled and cried. Momma and Poppa and their arms and legs grabbed and ran back and forth and up and down at each other and us. Momma and Poppa held us inside their hands and arms and hard so me and my bigger brother wouldn't go away again when Momma and Poppa let go of us.

Momma and Poppa told us they didn't want to miss us too. But there were other things missing from my little brother and people-family. But Momma and Poppa tried to put everything back where it was supposed to go again. Momma and Poppa picked my little brother up and laid him back down arms. Momma and Poppa rubbed their hands and arms together hard so they could dress my little brother's clothes back on to him until he looked nice and alive enough to go away with us again.

There weren't any nails to pound the top back down on top of the toy box hard but Poppa hit the top down hard and hard and down until it broke and stuck down hard. Momma touched the top of the toy box down too but it wasn't hard and she left her hands there. But me and my bigger brother wanted to put some toys inside the toy box with my little brother so he could go out and play for the rest of the way to Heaven and we would see him doing it when we got there. But Momma and Poppa told us we were going to sleep. We were going farther away and closer to Heaven but you have to go through the sun and burn or fever and sleep to get there.

Hendricksville to Bennetts Switch

Indiana flattens out and goes up on the map. America gets emptier the farther away you go up into it. Our car got emptier and our family did too. But we still weren't all the way there. It is so far away to go away but we could not stop yet. We needed to get to Bompa's house with as much of our family and stuff with us as we could. We stopped at houses that had families living in them so we could get some of their family away from them and keep going away.

We drove up into Hendricksville and down a street and up this one driveway that went to the back of this one house with a family in it. We stopped and parked and got out of our car and walked out into their backyard. My mother hung and pinned all my sister's clothes up on hangers and with clothes-pins on the clothesline in their backyard. All those empty clothes on the clothesline needed people to go inside them and wear them.

Their family came out of their house and their mother walked her little girl up to us and stood behind each of my sister's outfits that were hung up and pinned up on the clothes line. Their mother's little girl's arms and legs and hands and feet and neck and head all stuck up or out from behind my sister's clothes. That other girl tried all my sister's overclothes on—her church dress and the rest of her Sunday outfits, her winter clothes even though it wasn't ever cold in Mineola, her clothes for all the other parts of the year, and all the other clothes my sister ever wore over her underclothes and anywhere else.

Their mother's little girl looked like she was going to be everybody my sister ever was and my sister was going to be another size of girl and kind. My sister grew up more and more into the only things that were hers anymore. She got smaller like the small dolls of us that she made up of us. My sister got more inside herself after she got down to her underclothes and everything she kept inside herself so nobody else could take it away from her too. She got more family after the only things that she had left anymore were her her and her us.

My sister had to grow up into the one sundress she had left to wear. But my sister would only say how she was too hot and she took her sundress off even though it was the only thing she had left to wear over her underclothes or anywhere else. But my mother and father made my sister wear that one sundress out of Hendricksville and up through that part of Indiana where the rest of her clothes got us to Bennetts Switch. Our family was going to need everything we had left in it and us for us to get to Bennetts Switch and Frederick Perrytown and all the way to Bompa's house in Gaylord.

How Nobody Should Ever Wear Sun-Dresses Up to Too Hot, How Everybody Tried to Burn Me Up Inside One, and How You Make a Sun-Dress Out of the Sun Anyway

Momma gave all my clothes that were cold away to this other girl to wear them even when she already had clothes that were all cold enough to wear. Momma told me to wear my sun-dress all the way down over me even when it was too hot for me to wear it after the hot water springs or up to where the sun burns in the field or anywhere else the farther way up.

People need to wear either hot or cold or warm clothes anywhere they go but when your clothes are too hot on you then you sweat and something is burning up inside you. The sweat puts the hot and burn inside you out and you won't die unless you dry yourself off too cold. But clothes can take you away to hot or warm or cold for what you wear and how and where. But you can always undress yourself or wear some clothes else somewhere else and make your fever go up or down.

But my me wasn't going to wear my sun-dress or anything else over me but for my underwear. But you are only supposed to only wear underwear to go to sleep or down. But you should only wear my sun-dress only when you want to burn up. But don't wear all your new clothes together either or you will only go away to somewhere else you haven't been there yet and not where you're supposed to go away to or my little brother. Wear old clothes to go away to Heaven and everywhere else where you are supposed to go away to and wear them cold. Don't let anybody else but you dress you up or your fever will go up to too hot too.

You need to change more clothes more to stay anywhere alive and go away to bigger and to big-people. Momma still had all her clothes for me and her to wear so my people-me could grow up into her people-her and them and big. But Momma wouldn't let me wear her clothes anywhere else but where me and my bigger brother played Momma and Poppa and family. Momma and Poppa weren't going to play family with us anymore.

Poppa held me up and Momma pulled the sun-dress all the way down over me. They made my stomach and arms and legs and the skin all over all of them go up to burnt-colored where the sun-dress and their hands touched on me hot but they weren't going to kill me too.

They tied me back down into the sun-dress with a string at the back so your hands couldn't reach it and you can't get the sun off from you either. Momma or Poppa has to untie the string and let you go out of the sun-dress and the sun but they won't always do it. Poppa will put his hands all the way down into his pockets and Momma will close her eyes and go away. You are only supposed to die one at a time inside a people-family or anywhere else and we weren't there yet or me yet either.

Bennetts Switch to Frederick Perrytown

Everything gets bigger driving toward it—hills and curves and turns, telephone poles and the markers that count miles, the speed of other cars and the sides of long trucks, the roofs of houses and the people walking alongside the road. Everything else gets smaller driving the farther away from it. Bompa's house got bigger as we got closer to it and our house in Mineola got smaller the farther away we got away from it.

My mother got bigger and the new baby did too. My mother was going to outgrow her clothes like my sister and me did. My mother was growing a baby up inside her that was going to outgrow her stomach. Everybody that lived inside our family had lived inside my mother but for my father. My sister and me had outgrown her stomach and our brother had too but he didn't live outside her for very far away or long. My brother was back inside my mother and inside us too. My mother let us put our ear up against her stomach so we could hear him being alive. We could feel him inside her stomach with our hands and it felt like he could feel our hands back.

My mother's clothes were growing tight around where you could see the baby kick and hit to get out of her stomach and into our family. My mother had to stop wearing belts and pants. Her feet swelled up and she couldn't wear her shoes anymore. She kept getting bigger even though she threw up too. My mother was too big for almost all her clothes but there were other ladies that weren't mothers anymore or didn't have babies that made them too big to wear them. They all wore clothes without babies. They all tried clothes on out in the open and this one lady that wasn't going to be a mother anymore tried my mother's clothes on to see if they fit her enough to wear them out in Bennetts Switch.

That was the way that that one lady got to wear my mother's clothes and the way that we got from Bennetts Switch to Frederick Perrytown. We were going to keep going away and my mother was going to keep making another baby up inside her stomach. We didn't know if she could do it anymore but my mother was still going to try and switch the old and dead baby that was my brother for a new and alive baby that wouldn't die. Our family was going to need everybody we could get to live in it.

The Doll-Family Inside the Toy Box and How Anything Bad You Say to Them Goes Away from You to Them So You Can Go Away to Somewhere Else Better Than Where Everybody Else Is Dead

Momma and Poppa gave my doll-family back to me inside a toy box that was smaller than my hand. The doll-people inside my new doll-family were all smaller than my people-fingers. But the small dolls of us didn't have big enough ears to hear people-words. But you don't only always hear everything inside your ears. Sometimes you hear some things inside your head and mouth or stomach. You feel it inside you and you can't stop it from going inside your head. But Momma told me to say anything bad from inside me to the small dolls of us and it would go away from me to inside them and stay there with them so we could go away to somewhere else without anything bad else happening to us there too.

But my new doll-family was too doll-small to grow up into our people-family of us. Their doll-arms and doll-legs were made up out of sticks and pins that didn't move up and down or back and forth so they couldn't go away to doll-alive or live anywhere doll else either. Their doll-bodies were covered over with colored string and thread-skin. Their doll-heads were burned up where there should have been doll-hair on top. Their doll-eyes were poked out so the dark outside us was inside them. Their doll-lips opened up so you could see inside their burned-up mouths and how they yelled the hot back outside them and into the dark. Their doll-heads and thread-skin burned up and fell off their doll-bodies and down into their toy box.

But you can make a new doll-baby up by pulling on the colored string and thread-skin until it doesn't cover them doll up anymore and they are where we all are born without any clothes on them. Look down inside them to where they are sticks and pins for doll-ribs and doll-bones. Touch on them where their sticks and pins go across each other to hold them together or where there is a baby-clump enough of glue so it could be the heart. Cover them back up with colored string and thread-skin so you can hold the air inside them long enough to make them breathe and keep their people alive inside them. Make their eyes and lips go back to light and closed so they can look the dark back out of them and talk doll-talk until the words are big enough to be people-words.

You have to keep talking to them to make anything bad go away from you to them and not stop talking or it will come back and happen to you again or some more. Tell them not to leave any babies outside under the sun for too hot. Tell them not to bury any babies or anybody else or else you will have to go away to too far away to get them back. Tell them nobody else or family can have the doll-people that live inside your doll-family with you or your people-family won't go away together anymore. Tell them not to let Momma and Poppa or anybody else go away to anywhere else without you and Momma and Poppa will always stay there with you. Tell them you don't want to go away to live somewhere else when somebody else but you is dead and nobody else will die anymore and you can go back home. Tell them my little brother never got bigger enough to tell us how hot it was inside him and my little brother will get bigger and alive enough to talk to us and tell us what happened inside him and why he went up to Heaven and died. Tell them how many people can live inside your people-family and nobody will give you anymore people than my little brother to live and nobody else will have to die anymore.

Put the top back on top of the toy box after you stop talking so everything you told them will stay there with them. Don't stop talking or else everything bad else will stay inside you and happen to you more.

Frederick Perrytown to Edwardsburg

The car tires made this whining sound against the road that made the insides of the car and us shake. It could have been my brother crying in his room in our house in Mineola. It sounded that far away.

But my father would drive away off from the paved road and the sound would stop and my brother would go away. The car tires would make this lower dirt sound on the dirt road. The road dust would roll up behind us and the rocks would jump up and rattle against the underneath of the car or the rocks would hit the windshield and my father would flinch down but they didn't ever hit any of us. My father would drive over other things that had been hit in the road—dried animals that were already dead but that hadn't ever been buried.

We drove away and down and off that dirt road and up this gravel driveway and up to this house where this family lived. We knew there were people living there. We could hear them singing inside their family and house. That was the way this other brother and sister got the record player and the records my sister and me played with in the back seat. We'd spin the records around and around on the record player and with our fingers and our hands at different speeds until we got something to come out of them. Sometimes it was somebody and words and little bits of songs but some other times the whole music would come out too. Just don't push the needle down too hard or the point will break and nothing will come out that anybody else can make any sense out of it. You have to spin everything at the right speed and touch the needle down just right too. It will sing but you have to do it with your fingers and hands and listen down hard.

My sister and me tried to show this other brother and sister the way to do it but they said the records were only scratches and cries and then the record player stopped and was quiet. We showed them with more records but they couldn't hear them out loud. But maybe this other brother and sister got the way people heard us along with all the words and songs that were left in the record player and records that would play for their whole lives if they could hear them right.

But that record player and records, along with all those sounds and words and songs also got us from Frederick Perrytown to Edwardsburg. We drove through small places and little towns to get there. We drove past other roads where we could have turned off them and gone away to somewhere else. We drove through places that weren't big enough to stop at and the road just kept going through them. We drove under blinking lights where so few people drove through there that we did not have to stop. But the blinking lights made a clicking metal sound when you drove under them and we were going to keep going away until we couldn't hear it and you can't hear us or the way we talk.

How Momma Played Dead, the Shirt-Baby Poppa Carried, the Angels Inside the Clouded-House on Top of the Hot-Hill, and How Everybody Else Was Waiting for Us in Heaven

Momma played dead and the baby died again. Momma dropped the baby down out of her stomach and hole and blood. Momma wasn't going to carry the baby inside her stomach anymore. Momma squeezed words and breath out between her teeth and cried. Her stomach burned up and down and everything that was baby inside Momma came out of her and went away to where it wasn't alive anymore again. People and years came out of Momma inside clumps of blood that never got big enough or together and hard enough or skin-colored either. They never got eyes or nose or mouth and face enough for us to see the shape of a baby or my little brother in Momma's blood.

The baby was small arms and small legs and small head. It wasn't people enough to live inside our people-family. It was smaller than baby-sized and the other one of my little brother so Momma threw the baby away again. But Poppa got the baby out of the trash and wrapped it up inside his shirt for a blanket. The shirt-baby stayed together from how sticky it was inside Poppa's shirt and the hard way Poppa held the baby together inside his hands and blood.

We weren't going to bury this baby either. Poppa was going to carry the shirt-baby on the outside of him until it got big enough to be the little brother we needed for our blood-family. But Momma played dead like the baby did. Momma laid down on top of the ground and under our house-car. She wasn't going to go away with us anymore.

Momma told us to leave her there but if we did she was going to die outside there under the sun without us there with her. But Poppa got down under the house-car with her and talked to her with big-people talk. But he did it small and quiet. Poppa held on to Momma's arms and hands to pull her up and pull all the hot and burn and everything else bad that was up inside Momma back down outside her. Poppa held on to Momma's hands and arms and pulled on them until he burned his hands and arms up to too hot too. Poppa waved his hands back and forth at Momma and threw his arms up and down at the sun until Poppa's head and neck got burnt-colored too.

Poppa told Momma but Momma and Poppa only got hotter and hotter until big-people and angels came over and down. The big-people and angels stood up to cover the sun up and stop it from going up to hotter and hotter and burning Momma and Poppa and everybody else up too. It got darker and colder inside the shape of big-people and angels. But Momma told the big-people and angels to go away from us so the sun came back outside on us. The shapes of the big-people went away and down into the ground and dirt-world.

Poppa carried Momma into our house-car and drove us up to the clouded-house on top of the hot-hill. Momma and Poppa left our house-car doors open and ran away inside. Poppa carried the shirt-baby through the light-fire that was burning up inside the window-doors and Momma followed them inside the clouded-house.

Momma and Poppa left our house-car going but me and my bigger brother stopped it and closed our house-car doors so nobody else could go away or live inside it. We got the keys out of our house-car and got out of our house-car too. We went inside after Momma and Poppa so we could live inside where everybody is supposed to be alive.

There were more angels living everywhere inside than anywhere else but Heaven but we weren't in Heaven yet. The man inside the angel-colored long-coat wasn't God yet either but he goes anywhere anybody isn't supposed to die. He saves everybody's alive for them. But the man inside the angel-colored long-coat kept going back and forth past us and the angels were all going away to someplace else with somebody else but us. Nobody else or anymore angels could see us there until Poppa stopped an angel for us and told her to look. Momma told the angel she couldn't carry the baby inside her stomach anymore and blood.

The angel told Momma Momma had to hold on to her stomach and the baby and what else on Momma broke. The angel took Momma and us to inside a room and laid Momma down on top of a hard bed without any blankets or covers over it. The angel took the shirt-baby away from Poppa and laid it down to sleep on top of the wall-table and one more angel took the shirt-baby away with her to Heaven.

Poppa and the angel undressed Momma's clothes so they could dress her back up inside a dress that had a broken back. The angel looked up under Momma's new dress until she couldn't see anything else and closed her eyes down. The angel got out squeeze-clouds with rain water inside them and wiped Momma's legs blood-clean. The angel got the knife-stick out and pulled Momma's hair out of her hole. The angel walked Momma's legs up over her head and tied them up up there so she couldn't get away from us unless she walked sideways and up to do it. The angel pulled stretch-gloves over her hands and pushed a hat down over her head that had a light turned on on it so she could see if there was anything else still alive inside Momma. The angel poked holes inside Momma and her stomach and told her it hurt. The angel touched her fingers and hands and sticks inside Momma and pulled a handful of blood-clumps outside Momma that wasn't a baby or alive but that stopped Momma from dying anymore blood.

But when Momma wasn't going to die anymore then me and my bigger brother were going to go look for the shirt-baby that was going to live inside our people-family with us after it got big enough to do it. We went into and out of more and more rooms but everybody else was dying inside them. The big-people inside the more and more rooms were so much older and farther away than us that the angels couldn't always get all the way there to save them. The big-people were still alive but they couldn't get out of bed or move away to anywhere else. The angels tie you down to your bed with tubes that go into and out of your mouth and nose and arms and holes. Boxes with lights count your heart inside you and it doesn't stop going up and down inside your ears unless you pull the string out of the wall-hole. More boxes with more lights went up and down and away with small hills but they were too small for the big-people to go away and live on them.

The big-people drank bottles upside-down with their arms and breathed upside-down air-cups tied down on to their noses and mouths. The food they ate by pulling the table-blanket up over them and then going away to sleep under it until the angels came back for the trays and flies and bugs. There were more buttons that made them stop hurting so much. There were more buttons that rang bells and made angels come inside the room and get us. There were dead-tools that more angels poked more holes into the big-people with them. More angels dropped water and stabbed blood-needles into them with them. More angels cut skin-holes and pushed tubes inside you too.

But we didn't carry my little brother inside even one more room and do any of that to him or even give him to anymore angels either. We should have pulled the tubes out of the big-people that were older and farther away than us and pushed them back into my little brother for so far away until he got away to where he was older and bigger enough to be alive with us again.

We didn't want anybody else to die anymore but every time we went into and out of one more room everybody coughed and their breath went out of them. But we didn't breathe any of it back inside us on the way out of their room or we could have died from it too.

But where did Momma and Poppa go away to any older and farther away than us? But don't look for Momma and Poppa or anybody else alive down inside the basement. There were more dead people down inside the basement and there weren't anymore angels down there to save us. But look for more angels and they can see Momma and Poppa when you tell them you don't know where they are anymore. Angels can see things we can't even see even when we look straight at it. Angels know where everybody else is even when we can't see them anymore or they aren't alive anymore either.

Angels took our hands away from us and took us back to where Momma and Poppa were living at. More angels were going to look at me and my bigger brother and make us better than we were before we left there but we left there before they could do it. We had to go away again. Everybody else was still waiting for us in Heaven.

Edwardsburg to Sunfield

My mother lost another baby and we couldn't find our family anymore. We had to drive away again and some more toward Bompa's house to look for it. The only ways my sister and me knew about Bompa's house was from what my mother and father told us about it and from the family picture in the silver frame that had our whole family standing out in front of Bompa's house in it. Bompa's house was big enough for our whole family of all those people to live in it but none of them did anymore but Bompa.

Everybody in the family picture either died or lived somewhere else. My mother and father and sister and me all lived somewhere else even though my brother didn't anymore. There were also some old people in the family picture that were already dead and some others of us that weren't dead yet. The other people were my mother's or father's mother or father and their brothers and sisters and sons and daughters. They were our grandmother or grandfather and they were our aunts and uncles and nieces and nephews and cousins and some of them had dead brothers too.

My brother wasn't born or alive in the family picture in the silver frame. My mother was holding me up in the family in the family picture but my sister wasn't alive yet either. My mother had my sister living inside her but she was living with us in our family when we traded our family picture in the silver frame away from us to this other man that wanted our family. He took pictures of families and people and put them in frames and hung them up on walls. He collected families that way. He wanted to take more family pictures of us but my mother and father didn't want him to do it. We didn't need to remember anymore of our family than we already did.

But that man that got our whole long family in the family picture in the silver frame got our family lives. He got the family another way than us and our family got farther away. We left each place with less and less of our family and stuff but with the same amount of us. We got out of Edwardsburg and up into Sunfield. We went up through Schoolcraft and Vicksburg and Galesburg and Battle Creek to get there. You can go other ways there with a map but that way was the only way to get there with us.

The House with Counting-Doors, the Man that Knew How Many People Were Alive, Box-Rooms, More Holes, the Lady with the Rolling Trash Cans, and Why Everybody Has to Get Up and Live

The man that knew how many people were alive told us we couldn't live with him and everybody else inside the house with counting-doors. He wasn't going to count us up with everybody else even when Poppa told the man it was just for one nighttime. We needed to get Momma and us better than we were then but he wouldn't let us do it.

We stayed outside the house with counting-doors and looked inside the sheet-windows where we could see more people-families than us living inside their box-rooms. The sun burned the walls down so all the people-families were warm inside them. We could see through the sheet-windows and see how everybody lived. But we couldn't hear them say anything unless they broke their sheet-window open or bent their counting-door inside and looked outside at us with their bad eye. But we could see what they said on their mouths and faces and how they talked with their hands and arms. We could see it or hear it and it went inside everybody else inside the box-room. Little-people stop jumping up and down and hide under the blankets until they go away to die or sleep. Big-people climb on top of each other with their knees bent so their legs don't break. Everybody lives inside their alive until they go away to sleep and die.

You can live inside when you can open the sheet-window or the counting-door up and you can push and kick or pull or hit your way down inside it. The counting-doors push open or kick down and the sheet-windows pull out. You can push holes through the walls inside the shapes of hands and hitting or babies. You can reach through the wall-hole and open the door up from the inside to us.

We went away inside the box-room where there was a hole up high inside the counting-door and Poppa held me up baby to see farther out wide. But the man with bugs for eyes and blood for lips was outside and he pushed and pulled the counting-door back and forth until his long arms fell off and he rolled out wide away after them until you couldn't see him anymore. Poppa got the quiet down inside the box-room with his fingers and hands and holding them over our lips and faces closed. We talked with our hands and arms and hard and quiet until we went away to blind. But touch your eyes down hard with your fingers and you can see inside your head. Open your eyes back up and the colors will go out of your head and into the box-room so you can see again. You will see the bed and a wall-table, some wall-boxes that pull out, some places where you can sit down on them, and the wall-glass where the dark looks back out at you.

You can look back out the door hole when Poppa holds you back up baby but there wasn't anybody else out there where the living-world stopped for the nighttime. Poppa opened the counting-door up for us and we went back and forth to our house-car and the box-room. We brought our clothes boxes, Poppa's toolbox, and my little brother inside his toy box inside our box-room and locked the counting-door back up. Poppa got his short tree-fork out of his toolbox and Momma got some clothes out of the clothes boxes and laid them out on the bed. Poppa pushed the short tree-fork into the top of the toy box and Momma got the top off and my little brother out.

Momma held my little brother up inside her arms for baby and Poppa undressed his old clothes. Momma laid my little brother down to sleep on the bed and Poppa dressed him up inside new clothes that were bigger than he was so my little brother could grow up into them. Momma pulled one of the wall-boxes out of the wall and Poppa laid my little brother down to sleep inside it. Poppa opened and closed all the wall-boxes over and under my little brother and Momma closed the wall-box that had my little brother living inside it. The wall-boxes and the box-rooms are empty unless you can fill them up with your people and the beds up with your sleep and the places where you can sit down on them up with the rest of your lives and the wall-glass up with everything you can see when it looks back out at you.

But go away to sleep and it will be daytime again when the lady with the rolling trash cans knocks the counting-door down and gives you towels and soap. She told us we could take the window-sheets and blankets away with us so we could make a bed up and sleep inside it anywhere else we went away to but not there. She told us that that man that knew how many people were alive didn't start counting the doors and the people until everybody else woke up and opened them up and stood up inside the living-world with their people-family and lives. Everybody has to get up and live inside it for there to be a living-world.

Sunfield to Far Town

We drove away past these places where they burned little fires made out of wood and flowers on the corners where the roads crossed. We drove away past this other place where there were cars that didn't have any tires or doors on them and that didn't have any windows or seats or steering wheels or anything else in them. The cars were just car bodies that were stacked up.

That driving got us away to this house where this other father said he was going to take his family away from Sunfield and go away to somewhere else in America. My father told him he could have our suitcases, boxes, crates, and the other things where we had packed our stuff up since they were all almost empty anyway. But that other father and his family let us keep the things we had left in them—the underwear and the shoes, the doll parts, our dirty clothes, and some other stuff that nobody else ever wanted but us. My brother was the only empty thing that we kept with us. But that other family's car was going to be packed up with all the stuff they packed up in our empty things and all the people they had in their family more than us.

They were going to leave in the morning but they let us stay there that night in their house with them. They slept in their beds in their rooms and we slept on the floor and on couches and in chairs. We slept under tables and blankets and with cushions for pillows. We all slept through the night but our two families were too big for that one house.

We all got up the next day and we left when they did. That other family left everything else in their house but we couldn't stay there and live in it after they went away to somewhere else. We had to keep going away from there and everywhere else until we got to Bompa's house in Gaylord.

That other family got all our suitcases, boxes, crates, and the other stuff where we had packed our stuff up and that got us from Sunfield to Far Town. But there are more places to go away to than where we went away to and that other family that went away to somewhere else in America could have been us. But they told us they weren't going away to someplace else to live there. They were just going to see it and then go back home. But we couldn't go back home or stop going away from home. People kept dying and we kept going away.

That other family got so far away from us and the way we had to go away into our lives. They didn't have to take a dead baby away with them when they went away and they didn't have to make another baby up for their family and have it die too. That other family didn't have to fill that empty baby place up with each other and everything else that was in their family. But we needed to start our family and our lives

120

over again and we couldn't do it until we got to Bompa's house in Gaylord and started living there.

The People-Family that Had a Living-Baby Living with Them and the Way We Got Away with a New Baby of My Little Brother

Momma and Poppa stopped for us so we could go away inside the doll-house and play family with a people-family that had a living-baby living with them inside their doll-house. The Momma and Poppa there and their people-family had one of me and one of my bigger brother living inside it and their doll-house too. My bigger brother told me they were really real-family but we were only going to play play-family with them.

But we didn't need anymore real-people for our people-family but their baby of my little brother to live away with us. Me and my bigger brother took the baby and his bigger brother and sister into the little room where you make babies up inside it. They didn't have two babies of my little brother that were alive enough for my people-family and their people-family too so we pulled on this one alive one of him. We did it with his arms and legs against the other bigger brother and sister to see if we could get the alive one away from them or if they would get to keep it. But he stopped crying or even making anymore small noises so they didn't want the baby of him anymore when he was broken. The two of them that were us ran away from us and through their doll-house to somewhere else where babies aren't dead.

Me and my bigger brother ran the other way away with the baby of my little brother and outside. My bigger brother pushed the window up and climbed out of it and down on to the play-side of their doll-house. My hands and arms and me threw the baby outside through the broken window and my bigger brother caught the baby of my little brother inside his arms.

We undressed his clothes until he looked more like my little brother did and then we dressed him back up baby so he could grow up into my people-family and a better one of my little brother that wouldn't be dead anymore. We played more family with him. We fed him parts of trees and other big things so he would grow up bigger than he was baby and my little brother. We held the baby of him up baby inside our arms so we could be a Momma and a Poppa with a people-family where the baby stays alive.

We took the baby away with us so we could be the people-family we were before we left home. We took the baby out of their family so we could take him to Bompa's house and our whole people-family would be alive again. Poppa drove away and we got away with the new baby of my little brother until he started to die too.

Far Town to Morrison

There weren't any road signs for Far Town and Morrison but those places were there and we had to go through them to get to Gaylord. You can't go anywhere that isn't someplace. But sometimes the maps don't go all the way down to these small places and most times people and road signs can't tell you how many far miles there are to go until you get to them. But other times there are men with road signs that make you stop and go and men that put road signs up for new places and the ways to go to them.

We stopped our car along a Far Town road and we made a road sign up there and wrote Gaylord on it but nobody would stop and take us there. So my mother got everything from inside the glove box out of it and handed it out the window to my father so my father could lay all of it out on top of the car hood. My mother handed my father the maps and some other car papers, the flashlight, a pair of sunglasses, some batteries, a sewing kit, a first-aid kit, some gloves, and some other small things that could all fit inside the glove box.

My father told my mother and us that even all this stuff wasn't going to be enough for us to get away to anywhere else. But we weren't going to get away any other way anyway. We weren't going to need anymore of that stuff from inside the glove box anymore either. So my mother asked everybody that was going passed our car to stop and look at our stuff and us. My mother probably didn't know any of them but some of them looked like they remembered her or us from somewhere else.

Those other people looked at everything of ours that we put out on top of the car hood to see if they needed it or wanted it or anything else we had. This one woman took the sunglasses. This one man took the batteries and put them inside the flashlight and took that too. Another man took one of the maps to somewhere else and somebody else took another one of the maps to another somewhere else. More and more other people took everything else that was laid out on top of the car hood away from our family and away with them when they went away from our car and us.

All those other people got everything of ours from inside the glove box and that got us from Far Town to Morrison. The only things that were still holding us together anymore were the miles and the farther away and that we could keep going away even though we didn't have any maps anymore. We had to keep going away. My brother and going away were the only things that our family had left in it that nobody else could take away from us and that my mother and father couldn't trade away from us either.

How the New Baby of My Little Brother Started to Die Too and How We Gave Him Away to the Baby-Angel at the Hot-Hill

The new baby of my little brother wouldn't stop crying and we had to stop. His eyes were closed up so tight they cried and squeezed water drops out of them. It was blood-colored inside his mouth where his tongue made the crying go out of his mouth and into us. The crying went inside me through my ears and came back out through my eyes too. But Momma and Poppa told me to stop crying or this baby of my little brother was going to cry until its face burned up and he died too.

Momma and Poppa talked baby-talk to stop him from crying but he couldn't hear them do it. Me and my bigger brother made faces up to make him go away from crying to laughing but he didn't see us do them. Momma and Poppa made small noises go away from them and into him but that didn't stop him from crying anymore.

But he was going to die more ways than my dead little brother did. He spit everything we put down inside his mouth back up and out over Momma's shoulder at me and my bigger brother inside the backseat-room. This new baby of my little brother wouldn't even sleep anymore and it was going to break and stop and die from it too. But Momma told Poppa we needed to stop and rest or we were all going to break anyway.

We stopped at the same place where we were going to sleep again at nighttime. But it wasn't nighttime yet and nobody could sleep inside our house-car with the windows rolled up or they might burn up inside it. This new baby of my little brother would have burned up first but Momma got out of our house-car and carried him away to the water-room where it is cold inside there. Momma undressed his clothes and handed them to me to hold so he could fit back inside them when they were cold. He wasn't going to die anymore after he spit and pushed the burn and fever out of his holes where they smelled like my dead little brother did.

Momma dropped his legs down inside the bowl and pushed the water-button down so the water got cold all the way around his legs. Momma held on to him down and hard and he stayed with us after the water went away with the burn and fever that came out of him. Momma laid him down inside a smaller bowl and pushed the water-buttons down so the water rained down on him cold. He stopped crying and threw his hands and arms and water up on me and Momma too. Momma pushed the air-button down for the hot wind to blow out but it was too hot for him to breathe it inside him and not die.

Momma was going to hold him up until all the water dripped and dropped off from him. But Poppa got us back inside the house-car and rolled the windows all the way down and rolled us away from there. Momma reached him out the window and away from her and the wind held him up. His arms and legs and head went back and forth but none of them got bigger or broke off from him either.

We stopped when he was dry and cold and Momma dressed this new baby of my little brother up again inside baby clothes that weren't hot or sick. But Momma had to push his arms and legs into them and pull the hands and feet back out of the holes. Momma held on to this new baby of my little brother hard. Momma didn't want to let him go.

But we didn't want this new baby of my little brother to die too so we stopped at a hot-hill where babies and other little-people lived. Poppa took him out of Momma's arms and handed him to the baby-angel inside the hot-hill. There were more baby-angels for every baby inside there and they kept all the babies alive inside blankets. They laid them down next to each other inside long cribs and they don't pick any of them up even when they cry or reach their hands up.

The baby-angels keep babies alive even though they aren't Mommas. But the baby-angel that held the new baby of my little brother told Momma and Poppa that we were too big to live inside the hot-hill with them so Momma and Poppa couldn't leave us there too. But we were still alive and Momma and Poppa didn't want our people-family to kill us too.

Morrison to Gaylord

The men in the pickup truck drove up behind us and flashed their headlights up and down and close and far. They drove up beside us and rolled the window down and pointed us over toward the side of the road. We pulled over off the road and they pulled up behind us. We sat there in our car and they got down out of their pickup truck. One of them walked up on each side of our car and us. My mother and father rolled their windows down and they looked up and talked out to the men with slow voices. We all got out and stood in between our car and their pickup truck. The men touched us all up and down but we didn't have anything else with us but us.

The men got in our car and we looked at them through our car's back window. They went through everywhere in our car they could. The men went through the glove box and they looked under the dashboard. They looked in between and under the seats. They rolled the windows up and down and they looked under the hood.

The trunk was the last place where we had anything else left in it so the men opened the trunk up even though my father told them not to do it. They turned away and held their faces and turned back and reached around with their hands and arms. The men took the spare tire, the tire jack, the lug wrench, and some other tools out of the trunk and took them away with them when they left. The men closed the trunk up and popped the hubcaps off the tires. They got in the back seat of our car and pulled our back seat out so they could sit down in it in the back of their pickup truck. They took our rearview mirror too. That way they could see if anybody else was sitting down in their back seat. But we could still see all the way back to where we came from and what happened to us without the rearview mirror and we could also see almost all the way to Bompa's house anyway.

The men drove away with all the stuff that we had left but my brother and sister and family and me. There wasn't anyplace else for us to go away to but to Bompa's house. The men got all that stuff from inside our car but our car still got us from Morrison to up through Marceytown and Roscommon, on through Toms Mile, Bradford, and some other places that got their names from people that must have done stuff. My brother never got big enough to get a name but he was the last thing we had left with us when we got to Bompa's house in Gaylord.

How We Burned My Little Brother Up, How We Turned My Little Brother into See-Through Dirt, and How We Buried My Little Brother Inside a See-Through Jar and Farther Down into the Ground and Dirt-World

The fire-man was going to burn my little brother up until the fire turned him into see-through dirt. But the toy box burned up first. You could see my little brother through the toy box again but he was tired. He just laid there this time and burned up. My little brother's hair burned up and smoked his head. My little brother reached his hands and arms up to touch the hair fire out but his fingers wouldn't unfist and he couldn't reach it all the way out anyway. My little brother pulled his knees and legs up too but he couldn't walk or crawl anymore and the fire-man burned him down on his back anyway.

My little brother's clothes turned inside-out to burnt-colored and burned down into his skin. My little brother's stomach got bigger and bigger until his stomach got too filled up and hot and blew up too. My little brother's skin broke open until you could see down to his bones. You could see through the holes inside his face and down to the bone-color on his hands and feet and arms and legs and rib bones. His bones split up and he broke. His hands and feet broke off from his arms and legs and his rib bones split away from each other too.

My little brother glowed all the way down to his bones. But the fire-man was going to burn my little brother up until we couldn't even make the shape of a baby up out of him anymore. We couldn't put his insides back inside him. We couldn't put his eyes back inside his head or his lips back on his face. We couldn't pull his skin back over his hands and feet and arms and legs. We couldn't pull his skin back over his rib bones and everything else inside him or put his hair back on his skin or head.

My little brother was only small bones when the fire-man smoked the fire out. But you could see how sun-colored his small bones were burned. The fire-man can't burn the sun all the way back up out of you. But the fire-man can pick all the small bones of my little brother up and not even burn his hands up on them. The fire-man can make you even smaller than you were after he pours your small bones into an open bowl and pounds my little brother down into bone-dirt with a fat stick.

136

But the fire-man won't dig a baby-sized hole or bury my little brother down inside it either. The fire-man gives my little brother back to us inside a see-through jar. We buried my little brother all the farther way down to where you couldn't see him inside his see-through jar anymore. The sun couldn't burn him up anymore and the fire-man couldn't do it to him either. We buried my little brother all the way down inside the ground and dirt-world with dirt and rocks and everything bad else that happened to my little brother and us. We covered my little brother up with dirt and rocks and everything else we had left over over him even though it got so heavy all the way down on top of him.

Bompa's House in Gaylord

We drove up to Bompa's house and our family and our car stopped. The lights were on inside the house so we could tell there was somebody living there. We got out of our car and went inside Bompa's house—through the front door and the front room, into and out of a side room, along a hallway past the sitting room, living room, dining room, backroom, and bathroom. We went upstairs and along another hallway where there was bedroom, bedroom, bedroom, bedroom, bedroom. There was one bedroom more than there was of us but my brother wasn't ever going to live with us or sleep inside it. There was all this other stuff that also didn't have anything to go inside it. There were empty drawers and cupboards and chairs and rooms. But we didn't have enough clothes or food or people to fill a house up with a whole family living inside it.

We didn't have to unpack but we were going to be staying with Bompa in Gaylord anyway. Everybody else was leaving where they were living at too. Everybody else was driving over to Bompa's house to see my brother and us and the way we were going to live there.

They drove over from Traverse City and from Kinross and

from Clarion. People came over from Alpena and Arlene, from Black Lake and Walloon Lake. There were other people that drove over from Muskegon and Ludington, from Popple and Chesaning and All Bright Shores. People came up from Grayling and Lansing and Hastings and Plainwell and more people came down from Fenborn Quarry and Marquette. They drove their cars over with food and with babies and with other people with them. They had plants and flowers and trees. They looked at us and took pictures of us.

Everybody stayed the night. Nobody else died. Everybody else left Bompa's house but my brother and sister and me. Bompa stayed in his house with us but my mother and father traded my sister and me away along with all the other stuff that we had traded away along the way. Bompa got us and my mother and father got away. They were going to keep going away without my brother and sister and me with them anymore. My mother and father stopped living with us so they could keep going away inside the lives they still had with them with them. My mother and father were older where more things had happened to them from living so they had farther away to go away inside their lives than my sister and me did.

But my sister and me are still going to leave Bompa there in Gaylord since my mother and father left us there. We are going to leave my brother there too. He had already stopped and died and there wasn't anywhere else for him to go. But my sister and me had been going away for most of our whole lives so far and it was too hard for us to stop anymore. So we are going to go away from Bompa and Bompa's house and

Gaylord. We are going to go after my mother and father and everything else that made our house and our family up. We are going to keep going away for our whole lives and miles until we get our house and our lives and our family and our everything else that was ours back.

Why We Were Dead and Where Dead People and My Little Brother Go Away to Inside You

Momma and Poppa went away and left us in Heaven with my little brother and God so we were dead too. But dead people don't stay where they die. They go away too. You can't stop dead people from going away to somewhere dead inside you. They go away inside you and my little brother did too. They go away inside you through your eyes and away from there to inside your mouth. They go away from there to under your rib bones and down into your insides inside your stomach. They go out to your arms and your hands and your fingers until you can't feel them anymore.

But dying is going away anyway. You die when everybody else goes away inside you.